The Baptism of
Tony Calangute

Also by Sudeep Chakravarti

NON-FICTION

The Bengalis: A Portrait of a Community (2017)
*Clear.Hold.Build: Hard Lessons of Business and
Human Rights in India* (2014)
Highway 39: Journeys Through a Fractured Land (2012)
Red Sun: Travels in Naxalite Country (2008)

FICTION

The Avenue of Kings (2010)
Tin Fish (2005)

The Baptism of Tony Calangute

a novel

SUDEEP CHAKRAVARTI

ALEPH

ALEPH BOOK COMPANY
An independent publishing firm
promoted by *Rupa Publications India*

Published in India in 2018
by Aleph Book Company
7/16 Ansari Road, Daryaganj
New Delhi 110 002

First published as *Once Upon a Time in Aparanta*
by Penguin India in 2008.

Copyright © Sudeep Chakravarti 2008, 2018

All rights reserved.

The author has asserted his moral rights.

This is a work of fiction. Names, characters,
places and incidents are either the product of the
author's imagination or are used fictitiously and any
resemblance to any actual persons, living or dead,
events or locales is entirely coincidental.

No part of this publication may be reproduced,
transmitted, or stored in a retrieval system, in any
form or by any means, without permission in
writing from Aleph Book Company.

ISBN: 978-93-86021-96-0

1 3 5 7 9 10 8 6 4 2

Printed and bound in India by Replika Press Pvt. Ltd.

This book is sold subject to the condition that it
shall not, by way of trade or otherwise, be lent,
resold, hired out, or otherwise circulated without the
publisher's prior consent in any form of binding or
cover other than that in which it is published.

For Maya, flower child

Contents

1. The Professor's Guide to Vin d'alho — 1
2. Grace and Grief in Aparanta — 6
3. A Brief Aside with General Dantas — 16
4. The Baptism of Tony Calangute — 19
5. The Story of Dino and Ida — 25
6. The Life and Times of Winston Almeida: I — 34
7. And Casa Serena Goes One Into Two — 39
8. Aperitif for the Innkeeper — 46
9. The Life and Times of Winston Almeida: II — 52
10. A Crowd and the Innkeeper's Cross — 60
11. Old Acquaintances and a Princess — 65
12. The Life and Times of Winston Almeida: III — 72
13. A Little Something About Signs — 77
14. Dionysus Tells Some Folk Tales — 80
15. Great Games — 86
16. The Life and Times of Winston Almeida: IV — 91
17. Visions in Sodomo — 98
18. The Surprising Seduction of PI Fernandes — 105
19. The Life and Times of Winston Almeida: V — 111
20. An Audience with the Pope — 118
21. And a Little Bit of Closure — 130

22. The Life and Times of Winston Almeida: VI 134
23. Ida Gets a Tip from Highly Placed Sources 146
24. Dionysus Dantas's Date with the Fates 149
25. PI Fernandes and Dionysus Take Some Water 155
26. Carmelito and Caxinata are Acquainted with D. Dantas 158
27. When Does Ida's Hair Turn White Only? 162
28. All Souls' Day at Happy Bar 167
29. Aparanta Pokes Some People in the Bum 172
30. The End 183

Acknowledgements 185

1. The Professor's Guide to Vin d'alho

It takes a few twists and turns of tree-narrow lanes to reach the Professor, but those who make the journey through the village of Socorro Do Mundo by the sea rarely return disappointed. The Professor has a way with words, tall tales and short, and a touch of warm heart.

The journey will take you past the whitewashed chapel to Our Lady of Perpetual Succour. She is Nossa Senhora do Perpétuo Socorro to hearts lost in the mists of time. Or simply, Perpet Saibinn for those on intimate terms with the Mummy of the Son of God. That would suggest most of little Sodomo, as familiars refer to the village—for who does not make a wish to Mummy?

Beyond her place the palm-shaded strip of tar curves like a lazy snake, marked by a rough patch of grey-white stripes near the local grocery, Stanley's Homely and Timely Store. The patch was once an imposing speed barrier. It was levelled under protest, raised again, to be reduced to road yet again—though not completely, as if the goosebumps of tar and crushed stone would resurrect, as sure as the tides that shape this land, to slow down the impatient, belching buses on their way to the sandy terminus where the creek meets the sea. There, the buses wait a few minutes, while their drivers catch a breath of cigarette or gossip, or the eye of a fisherwoman, and then careen back with a cargo of people and fish over the little patch—raised or ruined—to transport Sodomo to the world.

Teofilo Pereira, Tefu to friend and foe, whose little house stands near this now-and-again barrier, worries that another part of him will come to grief—as an elbow and a shoulder already have—or, one of his pet mongrels will, in the rush of buses owned by 'dat fodrechea Nini Braganza'.

'Dey driving dere mummy's bum or *what*, men?' Tefu implores his wife Esmeralda, as every few months a mongrel does what mongrels do: chase mummy's bum and get squashed.

'When my doggy catch tief and save *your* bums, no, den okay, you pay me money or *what*?' Tefu eloquently argues before the village panchayat. 'Den, okay, *how* you let damn Braganza do me dis...dis-dat?' But his protests fall on deaf ears, and Esmeralda's prayers to the Saibinn go unanswered, because Nini Braganza generously donates many rupees to the members of the council of Sodomo and other territories upon which he imposes a swathe of lunacy, a monopoly strengthened by acts of generosity to officials in Aparanta's department of transportation and the police. This is overkill even for the Mummy of the Son of God.

Mostly, though, the faded stripes act as a guide for neighbourhood pigs to cross. And some that are careless when the buses come are rumoured to feature in the vin d'alho at Barretto's Bar and Restaurant (Established: Since Hippies) near the creek, buried in a misleading, all-forgiving pulp of tomato and vinegar and served to addled visitors from across the seven seas.

After another soft bend of the lazy snake, but before Barretto's and trance delights at Boom Shack, is the Villa de Vida. Here, at its Happy Bar, the Professor has just begun a telling.

◆

'Always vin d'alho, never vindaloo,' the Professor announces. Like an accomplished storyteller, he will not perform until there is an audience at the bar. Some are seated on high stools near the counter, others stand, or sprawl somnolent on cane chairs scattered around the large room, content to let the breeze carry words.

'Who would slay such lyrical language? Was it the British, or the Indians—it doesn't matter. I'm not suggesting we speak Portuguese, but does it destroy your soul, I ask you, to say "vin d'alho"? Taste the poetry on your tongue as you say it: vin-*dal*-yoh! Like a gentle wave. Barretto doesn't make it well, I tell you, and I have known of it from the time Sodomo was nothing more than a landing for fish, with not so many hotels that keep the sea from us. And, of course, fisherwomen in those days were prettier.'

The Professor waits for gentle laughter to wash over him, hooks his thumbs into the pockets of his blue trousers streaked with the silver of time and iron. He eyes his belly that surprises in an otherwise slim torso. ('As large as a budkulo, no?' as his indulgent wife, Magdalena Expectacão, tells family and friends, comparing this traditional mark of male well-being to the large earthen pot of Aparanta.)

'Now people from all over the world come to our tiny village,' the Professor continues, 'and turn a fisherman's hut into a hotel, and your Villa de Vida into a warm nest, may our sweet and lovely Perpet Saibinn bless us all.' The Professor makes a sign of the cross before resuming his tale. 'At the Villa we get clean gentleman-type meat, not from these poor creatures you see on the street. And the vin d'alho here is cooked the way my mother Agnes Constancia did—may Saibinn keep a kind eye on her restless soul—a little sour with sweet wine, so much red chilli to make our friend Lucifer sweat, and soothed with the finest pork.

'You should have seen her. First, she would cut the meat and cure it with salt and spices, without which it would not be Goan food. For us Goans the emperor of spices is, of course, cinnamon. There is a joke that we will sprinkle cinnamon on everything, even cinnamon itself, to give it more fragrance and flavour! My mother would take a touli and stir the meat with some mustard oil, and gradually add onions and feni—always coconut feni, the cashew feni my father would not allow out of his sight in fear we would drink it all, isn't it? Then some water, a little vinegar, and a lot of love. When our tongues watered like that of Tefu Pereira's mongrels', my mother would bring the vin d'alho to the table. It would make us forget our sorrows for a time. What a feeling, I cannot tell you, what joy to soak it up with finger-fat rice. What joy, my friends!'

The Professor stops for breath. Using the forefinger of his right hand he pushes his thick round glasses back towards his busy forehead, then absently rubs it on a chin merged with his throat. He reaches with his left hand to the bar top to take a deep sip of whisky and iced water, his lips making a moue on the glass. The hand delicately clasps the perspiring glass, little finger raised like a beacon. Straight out and all is well, a wiggle and it is time for another, Zezito the bartender knows. The Professor is as economical with movement as he is eloquent with words.

'With us, food is more than just something that helps life along,' the Professor resumes. 'It is life itself. It is what brings together the universe in a tidy serving on a plate. Of course, there must always be a little mango pickle and fried mackerel on the side, no? Ha-*ha*.'

The listeners smile. There is a giggle but the breeze masks its source and gender. Happy Bar smells of the sea and anticipation. It has smelt this way for as long as our genial innkeeper Antonio can remember and, swear on the Saibinn's succour, to him it sometimes feels like long enough. But he lets the thought pass, and with an absent-minded twirl of his fierce moustache, glistening like curved daggers above slightly smiling lips, looks without change in expression at the Professor's tableau.

'Ah, Goa,' the Professor sighs, sounding at once like a tired prophet and a man saddened by a straying lover. His eyes glaze over for some moments as he looks into his glass, his little finger makes a tentative wiggle, but not enough for Zezito to prepare a refill.

Ah, Goa. A tiny strip with endless ocean on one side and proud green hills on the other, the land in between basted with conquest from the time of the Mauryan emperor Ashoka to the patchy Pax Indica of lesser rulers, lesser still, in the frenetic churn of the new age that is upon us. In between, there was a long sabbatical as the Estado da India, a coveted ornament. The State of India was part of an overextended Portuguese imperial design doomed to failure—though not before spawning this beautiful mongrel speck on the vastness of a mongrel subcontinent, our Eden of half-eaten apples where we try so very hard to let people be as they wish to be.

But this must be more than Eden, Antonio thinks. Eden had only some apples, one serpent, one Adam, one soon-to-be busy Eve.

Did Eden ever sell its soul? Did it sell all hope?

2. Grace and Grief in Aparanta

But enough. There is time to return to the tales of the Professor and the simple pleasures at Villa de Vida. In Goa, once of the Estado da India initiated by the voyager Dom Afonso de Albuquerque, once Gomantak and Govepuri and, during grand dynasties of the ancients, Aparanta—the Land at the Horizon, the faraway land—there is always time. Sometimes, there is too much, what after a few drinks the Professor calls timelessness.

Aparanta has learnt to sell this timelessness, and tales of rejuvenation and trance, of be-as-you-want-to-be, by word of mouth, by ether. These are as powerful a draw as the forces that once brought conquerors from across the hills and oceans to Goa Dourada, golden Goa, for trade in spices, horses, men and women, religion and ambition, and made it a plaything of empire. Today, Aparanta by the sea is a plaything of the wealthy and a way station for the tired, the lonely, and convicts who carry with them prisons of their hurt. From this subcontinent and other continents, they arrive to marry into the discreetness of Aparanta. Others arrive driven by what Antonio's activist cousin Dionysus Dantas terms 'cheapery-buggery', keener on the destination than the journey, exchange-rate royalty who in a flourish of pound sterling, euro and dollar, seek out ever-newer conquests that permit planting of flags of the conquering nation at eateries. 'Charter Jack and Charter Jane,' Dino rails. 'Dregs even fucking Greece and Spain won't have any more, let alone fucking Portugal.'

Then there are armies of loud, littering Indians, eager for a swim, cheap drink mandated by a bribe of lenient taxation (the reward for Aparanta choosing India over Portugal), abundant ogle, and memories in one-wash-and-it's-over T-shirts.

There are others still, like the children from the lands of the Dead Sea, sickened, bleeding from sores, hating, frightened and confused, finding refuge in arrogance and trance, who leach into the gentility and greed of Aparanta. And the new Tsars with long-banished thoughts of hammer and sickle, ruthless, eager for conquest of a supermarket of drug-fuelled dreams, a state of mind that gives and takes so freely.

Antonio accepts that Aparanta is today, in the words of the lucid, ever-livid Dino, who has undertaken to rid this land of its ills, 'a painted courtesan'—and it is the destiny of a courtesan to receive those who will bestow on her what they wish: 'Some coin, insult, confusion, perhaps a kiss.'

◆

Villa de Vida is a small, simple, lovingly built puzzle of stone, picture windows and delicate balconies, the kind of place that forms only when heart is mixed into mortar. Pitted blocks of laterite are laced with plaster, gleaming white on rich brown. Ivy reaches out to balconies and snakes onwards, higher still, a green rush driven by sensory perception that, in a flourish of white and purple flower, annexes the tiled roof. Travellers come here to nest in simple whitewashed rooms with pretty curtains of floral print and little furniture, unlike the rooms so many of them have left behind, cluttered with their lives.

'Look after them, men,' Antonio's father, Francesco, had often urged, as he had one evening a lifetime earlier, during a few moments stolen between father and son at home, the Casa Serena, a sprawling paddy, grove of coconut and small hill away from the Villa. 'They have forgotten to live, forgotten to breathe. Some must learn again, no? Others must accept their failings, like someone who is drinking-drinking but cannot return via AA or slap from wife unless he accepts the path he chose was a wrong one.' It had sounded good, and his father was taken with emotion and a pour of cashew feni, so Antonio let it be.

Then Francesco declared for Antonio one of his commandments, as Antonio had known he would. Francesco's right leg, draped in delicate beige linen and perched over the other, had begun to swing in an increasing arc. 'How to go ahead, men, unless you know where to go from the crossing, no?'

Francesco and Antonio had been seated at the balcão at the Casa Serena—a place where Francesco usually declared his commandments—watching a line of ducks. They crossed the lane noisily, fluidly slipped into the pond in front of the house, and headed for the opposite shore at the eastern borderlands of Sodomo. The sun had retired behind the small hill. The quiet was loud here, merely a ten-minute walk away from the bustling beach lane of Sodomo. The sea would soon make its presence felt as winds washed through the fields, cleansing, reviving and preparing Sodomo for the dark.

There was talk of a sprawling estate being built here, over farmland and the patch of forest on the hill. Here, as elsewhere in Aparanta, the frenzy would move ever inland. In a few years, the space between the sea and the hill would likely be given over to homes and hotels for charter tourists, retirees from Europe, land sharks from New Delhi, the automaton beat of clubs and more peddlers of trance. So long as the village council continued to be led by Janardan Naik, who would stamp his approval on the sale of land for a consideration, Francesco and Antonio knew they could do little about it. And even if there were a way of stopping Janardan Naik, who could ever stop anybody from selling his own land, brought on by need, greed, or an estate fallen to disuse, the descendants of a family having moved on to urban lives in the subcontinent's rabbit warren of cities, or another continent altogether?

Till concrete came and robbed the sunset, the smell of the sea and the breeze, nature would continue to play at magic. At least, father and son agreed, Sodomo was fortunate in that it had only the sea and trance as draws; if it were further inland, between the rolling hills of Middle Aparanta and its eastern borders an hour's drive from the sea, Sodomo might have been nothing but crater and red dust. The lands of ore, open, spewing, insistent, covering forests and farmland and streams and wells with refuse from iron-red earth that is bounty for few and curse for many. The ores of Aparanta feed industry in the Far East. They feed, too, the great houses of Aparanta, which use the ore to flourish, to establish empires unquestioned by law and lawmakers. These home-grown conquistadors have little time for the wounds of others, of the land—a boon that feeds them and cloaks them in mastery. But the wounds of people, Francesco would insist, are always preferable than a land wounded by people. We heal quicker than our land. Such is the way of nature. Such is the Saibinn's way.

The poder had just been by on his creaking, rusted cycle, drawing Conceição the cook from the belly of the house with the insistent pom-*pom*-pom of the tiny bulb of a wind horn tied with bits of electric wire to the handlebar. She took delivery of flat poyee wheat bread and the family's favourite, undea, the hard roll with a soft heart that Antonio found so comforting with soup, roasted meat, wine, even milky tea. The ritual of the poder's arrival would not vary even in the rains, when trees bent with the fury of wind and water, when people were mere playthings for nature. In this mayhem, too, the price nature extracted for providing, the poder would arrive. He might be soaked, but the bread would be dry in the womb of blue oilskin. It was a compact of honour.

Francesco had waited until the poder had ridden away after his usual banter with Conceição. The ducks had wafted across, past the small white lotuses now done with their beauty business for the day, folding their petals, a chastity lock for which only the sun had keys.

'There is not much I can leave for you,' Francesco said then, between sips of the overlarge measure of cashew feni he permitted himself every evening, mixed with a little water and empathy and a twist of lemon, allowing the heavy, fiery liquid to work on his insides and make his blood run a little quicker. 'But if you look after these travellers—so like birds they are, no?—if you look after them like they were your own, more will come, and the Villa will grow like a happy tree.' He had then offered Antonio a drink.

'Obrigado, pai,' Antonio said, accepting, because he knew even his limited Portuguese reminded Francesco of the days Carmen, mother to Antonio, was still gliding through the house, gently chiding the servants, making sure everything was as clean as the lace she wove to half-cover windows, cascade over tables and cover her head at prayer.

Antonio could see into the house as he turned his head to the right, the doorway showcasing diminishing frames as they receded through the length of the structure, each successive door wearing an elaborate hat, one of coloured glass, another of curls of wood. The hand-painted azulejos on the walls of the sala depicting once-grand places of Portuguese Europe and the Orient—Lisbon, Macau, Goa—shone, the crystal glasses for port and liqueur and bone-china teacups in the cupboards looked as new as the day Carmen had brought them to Casa Serena as a bride. The dark wood of the delicate chairs and settees and cabinets in the outer rooms, with intricately carved vines and flowers, was shiny with reflection. Antonio then marked each object beyond the frame of coloured glass: one half of a darkly polished chest with a sunburst carved on it, two medium-sized Chinese vases resting on the top, and, above that, on the wall, a cut-glass lamp, now lit, the centre of the universe for a circular arrangement of small, exquisite azulejos. Just below the lamp hung a sepia print of Antonio's grandfather, Placido, dignified for posterity by Souza and Paul of Panjim—in stiff collar, string tie and a constricting suit of that age. Further down the hallway was a mirror. Antonio knew it well as he would occasionally preen in front of it, its heavy glass contained by an elaborate wood frame which ended in a gently curving top with a flourish of flowers that looked more like a coat of arms. It was all just so, the way Carmen preferred it, preserved now by Conceição.

Even in death, Carmen was ever present at Casa Serena. In the dark. By the light of lamps. In sunlight that streamed in through open door and windows, made gentle with tiny panes of crushed mother-of-pearl. In the long-ago days of Antonio's childhood, Francesco would often joke that his clothes were so well pressed he would be forced to walk ramrod straight even when drenched in pre-monsoon perspiration, or to survey the world like a lord in photographs and paintings even as he argued with fisherwomen over the price of mackerel or perch as he did on most mornings.

'You have made me into Dom Francesco,' he would joke with Carmen.

'What do you have left to conquer?' she would retort.

Antonio and his younger brother, Bernardino, would join Francesco in his gentle laughter, and the servants would smile their sunshine.

Antonio often wondered what loneliness had driven his father to destroy himself by choosing to be with Melba, may she one day feed the worms well. She would soon satisfy the creatures, he hoped, urged to their lair by the 'sleepy-fuck virus', as he had heard some schoolchildren describe HIV at the bus stop near the Saibinn's place.

Francesco and Melba had met at the bustling taverna she owned in Arpora market, at the crossroads of Sodomo and Saligao, the sprawling village to the east. Melba Bar & Restaurant, she called it, and Francesco had just to visit the childless widow—known for her prodigious beef roast, belief-suspending carnal appetite and ever-changing harem of young men, whom Antonio and Dino referred to as 'goats'—to be enamoured into foolishness. The goats were moulded alike, big-jawed, short-haired on the sides of their heads, curled and gelled cockerel mops in front, thick gold chains jangling with crucifixes over T-shirts that advertised European football clubs or American heavy-metal bands. Altogether, they gave the appearance of lost children that still suckled at their mother's breasts once before sleeping and once after waking. Now they had Melba, their mother superior, the teat of the world, Antonio would rage to the Professor and Dino at the Villa.

The marriage had been announced with the suddenness of a pre-monsoon downpour towards the end of May, a respite from sloth that appeared to dull even the busy wings of bees and flies. Dignity had prevented Francesco from solemnizing his wedding to Melba in the same graceful church at Saligao where he had wed his beloved Carmen; neither did he wish to shock Perpet Saibinn. He preferred instead to complete the vows in front of a civil magistrate in Mapusa. Gabriel Dantas had stood by as best man and witness, a sin for which Ida, his wife—Carmen's younger sister and mother to Dino—had not spoken to him for many months, but it had bonded Francesco and Gabru. Gabru had this once stood his ground and, over Ida's objections, Francesco would always be welcome at their Saligao home, the Casa Esperança.

Always the gentleman, Francesco had refrained from showing displeasure when Antonio told him Anastasia and he would be unable to attend.

The conversations between Francesco and Antonio had become rare after Francesco had taken Melba, the woman whose buttocks and breasts seemed to mask the horizon, as wife. To Antonio it was clear their width must also prevent the sun from entering Francesco's head to thaw the part of the brain that had the duty to keep a man's sanity from deserting him.

Antonio would later recall thinking, as he nearly choked with sudden blinding anger on that evening he had shared with Francesco, that while his father had moved on Antonio himself had resolutely preserved Carmen in his bedroom, in images framed in silver. It was a room that Melba, so overpowering after the diminutive and gentle Carmen, knew better than to enter, because even she knew what lines to leave uncrossed.

Francesco had seemed to read his son's mind.

'My Carmen…your mãe…' he had stopped.

Antonio, in shock at this overture, and out of respect, hadn't offered any encouragement for Francesco to continue. But Francesco, after a rattling sigh, had ploughed on: 'When it is time for God to claim me…' Then, in a burst of prescience, he had asked of Antonio a promise, intruding on his silence and their mutual worship of nature's magic. He was deeply embarrassing his son, he could see, but Francesco wouldn't be denied. He asked his son to be present at his funeral, along with Melba. 'Look into my eyes and swear on Perpet Saibinn you will do this last thing for me, because by showing her respect you will show me respect. I am paying the price for my mistake, but that is in front of God, no? If my mistake cannot be annulled on this earth, I must ask you to carry my cross, men.'

◆

The conversation had taken place about half a year before his second wife's madness for gold and younger men drove Francesco to Sodomo's pretty cemetery, a stone's throw from the Saibinn's watchful eyes and adjacent to the Charter Jack village of Calangute. And that was two monsoons ago on a day it rained so hard it seemed to Antonio all the green would run off the trees in grief. 'Even God cries for a good man, men,' the Professor had said in a choked whisper by the graveside, unashamed that some of the rain was born of him.

Antonio had reluctantly kept his promise to Francesco, but ensured that his father was laid to rest by Carmen.

Melba had left the funeral with her goats almost as soon as she threw a fistful of mud on Francesco's coffin, the pretence of marriage done with as it landed with a slap on wood already marked with wet. She had then held out her hand, palm open, for the rain to wash off the dirt, which had poured onto the coffin from her incongruously graceful fingers. Finally, Melba had fluttered her hand over Francesco's box to shake off the excess water. Even Father Gonsalves, 'pig intestine' as Dino sometimes referred to him, had the grace to look shocked, while Antonio's right hand reached out and gripped Anastasia's left wrist so strongly she winced, though welcoming through the pain her husband's first act of intimacy in months.

Ida, who lived in neighbouring Saligao and had attended the funeral in spite of her anger towards Francesco, had pinned Melba with a look she reserved for people she described as 'possessing serious birth defects, such as being born'. For a moment it appeared she would leap across the pit and attack Melba, but Antonio could see her being restrained on one side by Dino and on the other by her husband, Gabriel, and their little granddaughter, Anjali.

Melba's final humiliation of Francesco was somewhat mitigated when she stepped on a weak patch of earth near the arched entrance to the cemetery and fell on her ample bosom. Nobody moved to help, not even her goats, until they were energized by Melba's shrieks suggesting they copulate with their sisters, and if they were unavailable, on account of serial assignations with all males in the village, animals included, the goats could invite their mothers to bed. After a few seconds of shocked silence—it was within hearing of the Saibinn, First Lady of Sodomo, besides other ladies, gentlemen and children—for the first time in the remembered history of the village there was laughter at a funeral.

The mysterious winds of Aparanta that carried words would ensure the incident reached the furthest corners in a matter of hours. The passing of Francesco of Sodomo, gentleman and man of commandments, would be remembered for a long time.

3. A Brief Aside with General Dantas

Later at Happy Bar, the Professor, Antonio and Dino saluted Francesco's spirit. They willed him peace with a toast Dino had announced, just after his return from university in Bombay an age ago, for shape-shifting Aparanta. The toast had since become an anthem.

'Confusion to our enemies,' they intoned, as they emptied small glassfuls of feni warmed with fire and sugar down their throats, burning, soothing, banishing grief and the chill with this briefest of ceremonies. They would quickly pour another, because few drink only one measure of the essence of Goa—as rooted in life as a plateful of rice, fish curry, the monsoon and gossip. (And, as Dino liked to say, to Antonio's bemusement and the Professor's glee, 'as typical as the presumption of superiority that turns each slumbering village and town on their axes in goat-fuck denial of the world beyond their balcão.')

The newly wealthy of Goa eschew this brew, the mourners acknowledged, thinking their palate better suited to Johnny Black. But there could not be a true farewell with whisky, because a son of the soil must be accorded dignity on his final journey. So the best feni in Aparanta, from Siolim and areas further up the Chapora River and near the ore-laden eastern hills, had been obtained by the Professor, who doubled as the Villa's procurer-in-chief.

'It's the least we can do for Francesco, finally separated from his whore,' Antonio had said, 'Finally by mummy's side.'

The Professor had offered another explanation, using dialect that signalled there were no visitors nearby, in singsong English far removed from the actor-talk he reserved for the flock at the Villa. '*How* will a true Goan man's soul travel with whisky, men? God will take more tax from him when they shake hands, no?'

Dino had largely stayed out of the conversation, and continued to drink silently and powerfully, as he did at such times, surfacing from his stupor every now and then to pass judgement.

◆

'Cowed and cuckolded,' he said, describing Francesco to Antonio later that night after two pours of feni had turned to four, the liquid coursing down with barely a catch at the throat. Perhaps it was after five, for feni is rarely measured—it is either drunk, or not.

They had by now moved from Happy Bar to the shelter of Francesco's tidy office, now bequeathed to Antonio. It was too soon for Antonio to take it for his own. The old swivel chair padded with scuffed but lovingly polished green leather still had the slight indentations of what Antonio irreverently thought of as Francesco's bum and, as Antonio could not bring himself to obliterate the physical presence of his father, the three friends were seated on chairs in a row on the other side of the desk.

Dino's head was lowered, Antonio saw, his lean face and sharply manicured beard hidden by the curly hair he wore to his shoulders. Salvador Dantas in repose. If anyone but the Saviour Dantas had said what he had about Francesco, Antonio would have put a fist to his face before he could put the glass down to take a bite of chouriço. But Dino is different. He can tell Antonio things nobody else can. His heart is pure, and when it transports feni into his blood and frenzied brain, it opens windows in the attic of his head. After damning Francesco, Dino had swiftly, seamlessly, moved to his other incarnation, that of supreme leader of the Save Goa Society, his not-for-profit call to arms against the ills of Aparanta.

'It is good Francesco is gone. The Portuguese had been bastards to us, but apart from the Inquisition they had generally been civilized bastards. Today's bastards break our hearts where we sit. There would soon be no place to bury Francesco. You'd have to burn him and keep his ash in a powder tin in someone else's condominium.'

'To the land,' Dino had then raised his glass in a toast. 'To the people. To peace.'

When he spoke this way Antonio and the Professor would raise their glasses and good-naturedly call him 'General Dantas'. They knew Dino's anger wasn't as much against wayward travellers as those like Janardan Naik and 'high ministers and assorted official vermin', who lived on Altinho, the wooded, secluded hill at Panjim, chosen as the new capital of Aparanta after mosquitoes and disease had driven the Portuguese masters from Velha Goa up a single bend of the Mandovi, the same river that had ferried Dom Afonso a turn into the sixteenth century, and numerous fortune hunters who followed.

The rulers of Nova Goa—specialists in the compact that keeps the economy of trance alive in Aparanta by the Sea, tears ore for the world from Aparanta of the Green Hills and Forests and permits the land of the people to be converted to the land of the privileged in the Aparanta of Johnny Black—now live a couple of hundred feet above the busy avenue that skirts the sluggish stream of the Mandovi. It isn't very high, but it is high enough for those at Altinho to think it is still the seat of heaven and the spirit of the Inquisition never ended.

General Dantas presumes to challenge this empire. And as Antonio and the Professor know, General Dantas can sometimes be foolish.

4. The Baptism of Tony Calangute

When Antonio Placido Francesco Ave Maria de Sousa was younger, in the days Dino was yet to desert their childhood and travel to Bombay for university and Antonio was yet to come to the realization that if he attended another day of lessons within four walls he would like unkempt paddy shrivel and die, Dino and he would roar down to nearby Calangute on their motorcycles. They would weave like stunt riders around potholes and grooves of red earth yet to be elevated to tar-snake, scattering hippies, souvenir sellers and, sometimes, middle-aged and elderly visitors from abroad walking hand in hand with children who appeared to belong to bloodlines around Aparanta.

It was on one such trip that they had first seen Police Sub-Inspector Fernandes force gratitude from some bhaille shopkeepers selling trinkets near the beach and then move to an old lady from the village selling tender coconut, taking from outsider and local alike for the protection of the state. Driven by Dino's anger, the cousins had ridden up to PSI Fernandes and his small band of fellow law-keepers carrying batons and created a loud fence with their motorcycles. They hadn't said a word, only inched along to block the policemen when they tried to pass. A crowd had gathered, as it always does when a spectacle is brewing. A man staring intently at a puddle can bring Calangute to a standstill, and this was grander entertainment. PSI Fernandes had made the mistake of lunging at the tall and already enormous Antonio with his baton, but Antonio easily caught it. The more PSI Fernandes pulled at the baton, the firmer Antonio's grip became. The crowd roared in approval.

Having better sense than to try to take on a mob that was beginning to loudly question his parentage, PSI Fernandes had backed off towards his own motorcycle, all the while threatening to throw the teenage heroes in jail for obstructing police business. He derided their well-bred families as they would be able 'to do nutting, no, because…dis ting…Portuguese-type peoples no more bluddy-fucks rule Goa, no? So *how* you can, men?', and with a flourish of impotent baton, spat, 'Fuck-bastard.'

The encounter only made the cousins more determined. After several weeks of being regularly intercepted, PSI Fernandes left the small fish alone, preferring instead to concentrate on owners of beach shacks and Kashmiri handicrafts merchants, so plentiful along the stretch of road from Calangute to Sodomo that the cousins had christened it Avenida Srinagar. These fish could always be accused of violating zoning laws, procuring children, selling trance, and many rupees were to be gained in compact from a hundred real and imagined crimes. But even here, every few weeks, the policemen would run into Dino and Antonio.

Exasperated, PSI Fernandes gave Antonio the name of Antonio de Calangute, mocking him as if Antonio were a tiatr actor living in a make-believe world. The name stayed, because Dino later seconded with glee what PSI Fernandes had proposed in anger—much to Carmen's disgust, the bemusement of Francesco and Gabru, and the riotous pleasure of Ida. 'Tony Calangute,' Dino would snigger.

Unfortunately, Tony's younger brother Bernardino could not participate at this rechristening, having already been 'called away by the Lord', as the family announced in the obituary pages of *Goa Chronicle*, which made a tidy profit from such final journeys. Young Bernie, on his motorcycle, had been clipped by a bus full of wedding revellers on the narrow, winding road at the nearby village of Pilerne on account of the bus driver—the groom's cousin thrice removed but close enough to be counted as family as such things are in Aparanta—preferring to participate in the celebrations, from roasted pigling to counterfeit Johnny Red.

It was as if Bernie's death marked a departure for the cousins as well. Dino had soon after left for Bombay, treading the path of generations from Aparanta who would seek out opportunity and employment that their home could rarely provide to those without an interest in tourists, land, ore and rule. But Tony always felt that Dino's growing anger against the rulers and abusers of Aparanta, far more than his pursuit of a career, had driven him away. It had brought Dino back as well, on-edge and confused, a promising career in finance given up to rail against all establishment, and expecting everyone to join him in retribution and upheaval. Save Goa with the Save Goa Society. It was as if only Dino could provide succour, as if nobody else cared.

'But how can I tell all this to a man who is both brother and friend?' Tony had asked of Anastasia, when she had once urged him to counsel Dino soon after Francesco's passing.

'That's *why* you can,' she had replied with calm logic. 'No job, wife gone, a child to bring up—*I* look after her more than he does. Anjali is hardly his daughter any more. She is everyone else's daughter. She is like my own...' Anastasia had stopped, in a boat stranded in midstream, adrift, unable to reach shore, admit to a numbing truth, and stared at Tony like a trapped animal.

'His mother can tell, no?' Tony, cold to the pit of his stomach, had attempted to sidestep the issue. He discovered his fingers frozen in the act of buttoning up his shirt.

'She won't, because he is too much like her, don't you see?' Anastasia had spoken gently after an age, with the voice of an old woman. 'What Ida cannot do, Dino must, no? I love Aunty Ida like my own mother, and Dino is Dino, but how Uncle Gabru can deal with both her and Dino I don't know.'

'Dino will calm down.'

'It will be too late,' she whispered, turning away. 'Goa has never had time for saviours, only martyrs.'

Tony had remained silent. To fire, his answer was peace and compromise. As far as he was concerned, his only act of rebellion, against PSI Fernandes, had been a bad dream best forgotten. He could only try and do the same with the stories Dino carried with him like poison arrows; and the disquiet brought by Anastasia's grief.

◆

At Villa de Vida, practising a commandment of Francesco, Tony tries to ensure that 'to live life most fully and relaxed, men, walls must not be walls, and time not time, no?'

Accordingly, the innkeeper welcomes birds of many feathers at the Villa, especially the ones that are hurt, easy to distinguish because they have a look in their eyes, tired and frightened, like they cannot fly any more, away from their world or themselves. They come here to mix the promise of Aparanta with the Villa's warm sparseness, to offer themselves to the god of renewal, allow newness to be composed one grain at a time like the dunes across the road, the past over, the future an idea. Often, their few planned days at the beginning of in-migration after the monsoon deluge spontaneously extend into weeks or months. Like Francesco before him, Tony never denies them. Some birds come even if it is the wrong season for migrating, when an overdressed army in grey-black marches across the sky and the sea loses its hard-won calm of blue and green to mud. The army has many names: monsoon, water of life, succour, peace. Four months of rain that cleanses dirt and the cluttered mind, charges aquifers along with the soul. It is a time for the renewal of the species, for Aparanta to shed skin.

Over time, picking out the wounded has become easier for Tony: if they have pride they look quickly away because they know their eyes will, at the point of contact, reveal weakness and they will lose what dignity they have left.

But in the early days Tony could not always pick them, as he sat by Francesco, helping the newly arrived fill a form for a room at the Villa. Every day he would drop by the Villa on his cycle on the way back home from St Joseph's—not an easy task if Brother Dominic had taken a cane to him, though that was only every two weeks or so, a grand record of conduct compared to many others in his class. Certainly better than Dino's, whose posterior and knuckles were so raw from visitations of Brother Dominic's cane that the headstrong Ida had one day dragged Gabriel to the school to confront the padri with a string theory. Had he a disturbed childhood? Perhaps abuse at the hands of an uncle, or beatings and worse from a drunken father? Or maybe ministrations by a padri, not unlike him, who took advantage of women and possibly some men at confession? Only the direct intervention of the bishop, a friend of the family intimate enough to refer to Ida's husband as 'My dear Gabru', ensured Dino did not have to either change school or suffer more beatings. It had also helped that Gabru had considerable influence as a senior lawyer of impeccable standing and a lineage that could be traced, give or take a few branches of the twisted tree of life, back to the dalliances Dom Afonso had ordered his officers to undertake with fair-skinned widows and daughters of 'Moorish' occupiers of Aparanta. (Their menfolk the Dom's troops had slaughtered to plant the seed of Portugal.)

It is October now. The army has retreated, and the flock has begun to arrive. Brown is washed off the sea. The breeze merges the sound of stirring coconut palms with that of waves. It is a sensation Tony knows well, with closed eyes it is easy to imagine being covered with ocean while being dry in the shade. 'Open your eyes and it would instead be the wind that covered your body like a lover,' Anastasia had said in their days of fire, when Tony was filled with her words and her slender, elfin beauty, as they reached for each other.

Now, there is a dull ache of emptiness.

Maybe I am a small man, Tony, the orphan, thinks. Too small for the perseverance of even a small innkeeper, too small to gather up a life, too small to not smile for my earnings, too small to understand Dino's rage, too small for the grief and longing of others.

When the ache becomes unbearable, Tony quietly takes to space, away from Casa Serena, away from Villa de Vida, alone by the sea that embroiders the land to the west. At these times the Dom visits, politely entering through doorways in Tony's mind. There is little he can do about it, and sometimes it is even a relief. The Dom, more alive in death than Francesco when he was alive, is now father, confessor, friend.

5. The Story of Dino and Ida

Those times and other memories are occasionally relived as the friends would do unto themselves, away from the confines of the Villa, even forsaking its heart, Happy Bar, for hideaways like the tiny no-name hut in Parra, north of Sodomo, kissing the narrow winding road to Mapusa that Tony, Dino and the Professor maintained served the greatest shark ambot-tik in all of Bardez taluka, mixing sour with the smell of sweet earth and rain. Frog Bar, the friends call it. Shared space.

Fed and watered, the friends would look at the distant city lights of Mapusa, which appeared sometimes to disengage and drift towards them, gradually transforming into onrushing headlights they would stare at like brazen prey. When these too would pass, they would sit silently in rapt worship of nature, fêted with an impromptu concert by delirious amphibians.

The time of the hippies was not free of trance, they remember. The flower children smoked ganja or charas and licked LSD from strips of paper. Many took flight on heroin. Tony had heard that rock stars from England and America would sometimes be among them, mingling incognito like kings and queens in a crush of delirious peasants. Throes of that liberty laid the seeds of the later trance empires of Aparanta, but in those early times the day appeared in no hurry to retire. There was still respect for others, for Aparanta. Now time passes more quickly, with more urgency, 'like paradise trying to put in overtime', as Dino said one evening at Frog Bar, and Tony and the Professor sat mute, refusing to allow Dino's rant to come in the way of their contentment.

These days, revellers will eat and smoke anything, Tony suspects, even goat-shit dipped in feni which that snake Mahboob Butt sells from his handicrafts shop at Boom Shack at the Sodomo end of Avenida Srinagar, a shout away from the Villa. Although, from what Tony hears from Dino and some of the boys, MB, as Butt introduces himself to travellers, especially female, doesn't need to sell goat droppings masquerading as hashish. The supply of every imaginable narcotic known to man is plentiful; there is a menu, verbally shared, once MB has gauged the need. It is fuelled by a chain that stretches across the length of the Himalaya and more, eastwards from Afghanistan to Myanmar, a southern chain reaching through the megalopolises of Delhi and Bombay, trance hamlets of Manali in the mountains and Pushkar in the deserts of Rajasthan, and on to Goa. The natural and chemical produce is even more prized than fresh saffron from MB's beloved Kashmir, as coveted as caviar from the dying Caspian, and fought over by many, including Russia—the newest superpower in the commerce of trance.

Increasingly, Dino does not wait to be away in no-name havens to show anger.

'Forget tit-ogling Indians,' he growls. 'Even Goans can't get to their beaches now. It's like the Republic of Freakonia out there.' Tony brays with laughter. Sometimes it's a treat when General Dantas is angry.

They are at a corner of Happy Bar. It is late morning and, between meetings of the Save Goa Society and daily plotting of revolutions against demons in the land, demons in his head, Dino has already travelled through two 'half-quarters' of feni, a third just tasted.

'When you can get your mind away from making money and searching for a perfect life,' Dino continues without missing a beat, drying up Tony's mirth, 'take that damn jeep of yours and go see a few places in your beloved Goa.'

Tony is now concerned. He has told Dino many times not to come to the Villa during the day, when his mind is on guests, the Villa, a hundred other things, but Dino has not been himself the past year or so. He is angrier than ever, and his anger is directed at everyone and everything—'political worms, ore-sons and un-real estate developers' and other conquistadors of Aparanta's land, trance merchants, the overflow of travellers, the ennui of residents, himself. The anger is as indiscriminate and insistent as monsoon rain, wetting everything, the water finding places to travel to like air, dampening the skin and bones of people and houses. Like a petulant child-man, as it appears to Tony, Dino cannot accept that people will make accommodations for wealth. That the democracy that swept over Aparanta like a wave when the colony planted by Dom Afonso in 1510 became a colony of India in 1961—in the days Dictator Salazar of Portugal banished free thought, and India, a child nation, was still learning to think—also brought with it other facets of indelible right.

'Everybody has the absolute freedom to be corrupt,' General Dantas is deep in his spew. 'Everybody has the absolute freedom to poison the land. Our leaders have the right to be thieves. Every fisherman and toddy-tapper's son now has the freedom to wear a Manchester United shirt and fly flags of any country that will give us bread—Oi mate! Freund! Tovarisch! Our daughters have the freedom to be passport whores. Look around you. Goa is solid-fucked. Look at your neighbour. You think that bastard MB only sells furniture at Boom Shack? I'm going to shut that bastard down! Him and his whole fucking chain of shut-up-and-pay-up, right from Avenida Srinagar to the see-no-evil motherfuckers on Altinho.'

He resumes after a brief pause, hardly out of breath. 'That Butt fellow… you know he sells drugs, don't you? I sent Vijay from the office dressed like the trash-boys, unshaved, beads, headband and all, and Butt gave him a complete rate list—hash this, cocaine that, meth, ecstasy, ketamine, what-not. He even told Vijay, when Vijay pretended to be nervous about the police, that the police are in his fucking pocket.'

Tony acknowledges that he has heard MB sells trance, but as nobody ever told him they had bought anything else in his shop except overpriced jackets, carpets and furniture, how would he know. 'I don't ask my guests what they do, as long as they don't create trouble for me.'

'That's the problem with you all, brother mine,' Dino attacks. 'Eyes closed, ears closed, mouth closed—happy fucking monkeys. Houses across your precious creek leave their trash on the sand and behind rocks at low tide. The fields behind the Villa are planted with plastic bags and junk. Do you even see? You're all dying, and you don't even know it.'

Dino knocks his glass over with the sweep of an arm. It shatters on the floor and Zezito rushes to clean up. It is good Happy Bar is empty except for the three, as Dino, even if temporarily spent with his anger, isn't finished.

'When the land you have loved from childhood goes to hell, just to open your eyes is to be angry,' Dino lowers his voice, forcing Tony to lean forward for the words. But Dino could be talking to himself. 'If there still wasn't beauty in sunrise and I did not wake up with birdsong, I would either leave this fucking place, or take some of the bastards with me before I die.'

The innkeeper is quiet; anything he says will only stoke his cousin. To Tony, Aparanta is like an island, and he plays his small role as islander, letting the surge of travellers and ideas arrive and depart with studied disregard. But Dino challenges the security of isolation spurred by fear and the island-smallness of mind that curbs Tony.

'You have enough to do,' Tony says after several minutes, unsure if this will set Dino off again. 'How much can you do on your own?'

Dino angrily shakes his head, and is then distracted; he stares automatically at the legs of Sally, who has just walked in. Tony does that himself sometimes, with Sally and others, but not for long, because a commandment of Francesco isn't far: 'Keep your eyes straight and your snake in the pants, men, because going to confession will not fool Perpet Saibinn into forgiveness, no?' It is a helpful commandment, for temptation is a bastard of an emotion. Tony doesn't want to lay claim to it, even though what he has with Anastasia is like the fading picture of Lisbon in the veranda of the Villa, a souvenir of Francesco's last visit to the city before Liberation.

In the short silence, words float into Happy Bar. Umesh, the major-domo, is gently telling Babu the gardener his father is a dog and his mother a hen so it is only natural that he doesn't know whether he should piss on the bird of paradise or lay eggs by the jasmine. The fool has planted spinach along the rows on either side of the gazebo near the small pool instead of at the back of the kitchen near the well as Umesh had so clearly instructed. Sally, now seated near the door, is smiling; Umesh speaks in Konknni, its singsong is strange and beautiful even if she cannot understand a word.

Dino reluctantly looks away from Sally, and resumes his attack. 'Animals!' He bangs his fist on the bar top, startling her.

Tony smiles in apology to Sally, and tries to change the subject to calm Dino. 'So tell me, what's new?'

'Fine, I'll stop,' Dino sighs, hands raised in retreat. If he had started this at home, Gabru would probably have called him 'estúpido', and given him an earful about his refusal to do some 'proper job like a civilized gentleman, not this running around and all trying to save the world'. He would perhaps have added a plea, unmindful of Anjali's presence, agape at this public upbraiding of Dino-daddy: 'What *for*, baba? Will God give you a double MA? Isn't it enough you are doing number one on what you learnt?

Who will look after Anjali after your mummy and I are…called away by the Lord?'

Dino would have glared at his father, mute with rage, and gradually softened as Anjali took him by the hand and led him from the room. Father and daughter would sit in the shade of the jacaranda or jackfruit tree, and be soothed by the bougainvillea jewels that protected Casa Esperança, the house of hope, from the eyes of Aparanta. For a time, a child would will peace.

◆

Dreams lay beyond the ocean, stretching past the Arabian Sea to the shores of Africa, the destination of so many sons and daughters of Goa in the days of empire, chasing futures in Portuguese dominions and beyond. Ida and Carmen were daughters of Mosmikar, bloodlines that had travelled to Mozambique. Perhaps that is why they were always able to keep their distance from Goa even if they had chosen to marry and die here—as he would one day in modest Sodomo, Tony often thought. This is home, even if Anastasia increasingly nudges him from it, insisting they will recover their lives if they move away from Melba's pestilence.

Ida and Carmen had distance protected by grace and charm. It gave them a dignity the local-born often hated because the sisters remained aloof, while they waited for Ida and Carmen to ask to be included in the incestuous folds of Aparanta. The sisters required no props of acceptance, and cared little—Ida less than Carmen—about how many drops of Portuguese blood suffused them. Over the years, Ida's resolve to retain her independence had grown stronger, manifesting itself in ways that would filter down to Dino. Father Gonsalves, who ruled over Saligao, the sisters' home village, and had visiting rights to Sodomo, was not welcome in the Dantas household. No padri was, for that matter. 'I have enough trouble cleaning out mildew after the rains,' Ida would say. She also treated the other institution, the panchayat, with disdain, saying it was largely riven with greed, and would override every objection Gabru voiced as he urged Ida and Dino to be realists.

'Advogado Dantas,' Tony had heard her tell Gabru once at a family lunch on Sunday, 'you worry about the law and you let me worry about dignity.'

Carmen had been alive then, and Tony had seen her hurriedly cover her face with a napkin, as Francesco minutely inspected his glass of Alentejo and Gabru went red in the face and savagely pushed a silver spoon with a carved ivory handle into the crust of his portion of baked fish. The thin but hardening cheese resisted for the briefest moment before giving up an unequal fight; but then cheese never fights back.

Embarrassed, Tony had averted his eyes and looked at a neutral space; a convenient one was a five-tiered triangular stand like an ebony wedding cake, wedged into a corner of the room, its twisted columns supporting a number of Chinese teacups with lids, and small bowls. Then, feeling particularly intimidated by the oppressive silence that had descended over the table, he looked to the windows and for a while was blinded by the glare, better able not to see and therefore, as his mind urged, less able to hear the rage around him. But how does one disregard Ida? Unrelenting, she had continued, 'I shall not allow vermin into my house as long as I live. There is no place in this house for priests and politicians, and there will never be. We need God, not travel agents of God, and certainly not carrion eaters pretending to be leaders of people.'

Little Anjali, seated next to Anastasia—Nasty-mummy in a yearning child's shorthand of affection, and the cause of good-natured teasing in the family for Anastasia—had looked wide-eyed at Granny-mummy, so different now from the lady who told her stories and taught her to imitate the koel that ruled the large flame of the forest behind the house. Little dalliances that made her forget that her mother, Christabel, was now in Melbourne with another man—a generous 'Dubai-returned' man from Chandor who had gladly given her mother the baubles and comforts Dino, whom Christabel had married in the hope of an urbane lifestyle, at the very least in Bombay if not other cities of the world, would not.

Anjali was too young to understand Granny-mummy's fury, fuelled by the advice Father Gonsalves had given to the plump and pretty Christabel, suggesting to her a way out of her unglamorous marriage while keeping intact the sanctity and order of the church. It would be accomplished with the simple expediency of conceiving a child from a lover. 'Any man, men, *what* matters? But you're lucky, no, to have Xavier loving and all dat?' If Dino wanted to keep their child, Father Gonsalves had explained, it was all right, as Christabel would now have a new life, and that too was the will of God, no? Christabel had announced the coup to Ida as a fait accompli when Xavier's seed had taken hold. By the end of that day she had removed every trace of herself from the Dantas household and left for her newly beloved's, in his lily-white Mercedes, with a hurried kiss for Anjali, who had reached out and discovered a receding car.

Soon after, Anjali earnestly took to her search for mummys, as Dino did to protest—both fortified by Ida, and Dino also by drink.

Perhaps the restless spirit of the Mosmikar is stronger in his blood than mine, Tony sighs, remembering the admiring look on Dino's face as he glanced at his mother across the table on the day Gabru won his battle with the cheese. Over time, Dino had added two others to the hate list Ida espoused, calling them the 'four Ps of Goa: politicians, priests, pimps and pushers, but not necessarily in that order, no?'

'The bonkmar in Altinho are playing their games again,' Dino says after a few minutes, his eyes back on Sally. 'The bastards are going to open up more coastal land for construction.'

Tony is curious. Laws got customized from time to time in

Aparanta, but in the past few years the frequency and magnitude had increased.

'Number One is allowing it,' Dino elaborates between sips of feni. 'North of Chapora. The whole bloody virgin stretch from Morjim to Keri. Whatever's left in Dona Paula. Forest land in the interior—anything at all. And our friend Winston Almeida now wants north Goa. The south has become too small for him. We've got to stop that pigfuck-bastard.'

Tony winces. Winston, who is like a crow, intelligent and without conscience, hates to lose. If Number One, the despot of Aparanta, is on board, as he is with anything bigger than the salaries to sweep Church Square in Panjim, Winston will walk as a lord, Visconde Almeida of Nova Goa. And where evil walks, Dino will follow, feverishly rallying opposition with his cohorts at Save Goa Society—whether they wished it or not—placing passion before practicality.

If that came to pass, Winston would surely visit, Tony knows. They all came to reason with Tony mistakenly assuming that the innkeeper's diplomatic streak might work where cold logic would not, because incestuous Aparanta knows if there is one person Dino is likely to listen to other than Ida, it is Tony. And so, Tony may have to face Winston with a smile on his face when all he wants to do, as Dino once did and lived, is spit on his face.

6. The Life and Times of Winston Almeida: I

There are stories in these sands that drape the coast like a wedding sari. There are stories in the waters that nourish this land. There are stories in these seas that once shaped the history of the world. Everyone has a story in Aparanta, grand tales of profit and loss.

And that is how we visit Winston Almeida, aspiring thug lord of Aparanta, beloved son of the late Olimpio and Fatima Luisa; belligerent and straying husband of Lumena; doting brother of Gilu (Guilhermina), Filu (Filomena) and Pilu (Pilomena)—because Olimpio and Fatima Luisa expected Winston but were instead constrained to rhyme; demanding brother of Franklin and Iosif; and overbearing father of Tojo, Tito and Tarzan.

There are those who look to Winston's DNA to gauge his streak of obsessive behaviour. And they would be correct. After all, Olimpio had been a strange cauliflower even as a child, steeped in fantasy and an extreme form of idol worship. Stranded in the tempestuous 1940s in blissful Goa under the neutral Portuguese flag—as neutral as flags could be, at any rate—the teenaged Olimpio Almeida had felt left out of the grand events shaking the globe. The future headmaster from Varca on the southern coast of Aparanta would clandestinely listen to transmissions of the Bombay station of All India Radio at home, about the valiant defence of Britain, Japan's stealthy bombing of Pearl Harbour and the subsequent outrage of America's crippled but adamant president. There were reports of fighting on beaches and in deserts, the drama of the epic battle in the sands of Africa where the craft of Montgomery demolished the genius of Rommel. Stories of the Soviet Union's heart-rending defence of the motherland moved Olimpio to tears. Only much later did he hear of Stalin being denounced for strategic silliness that had led to the grand defence in the first place, and the butchering of millions of Stalin's own people. But Olimpio dismissed it as irrelevant data urged by Russian feni, as it were, especially as the denouncements came from the bald successor to the fiercely hirsute Stalin, with a woman's name, Nikita, to cap it all.

Driven, Olimpio commandeered a length of blood-red cloth his indulgent mother kept to make dresses for children who attended Red Rosary School. The next day, he broke into the store of his modest school, St Alex Preparatory, and discovered tins of white paint. Finding a tin partly open, Olimpio took it as a sign of divine complicity. Not sure how to place the hammer and sickle, he painted them with a coir brush side by side in one corner of the cloth, and looped a couple of his father's pyjama strings through clumsy rents at one end of the cloth. He then sneaked up to the roof of the school and hung it from the cross, delighted to see the red banner unfurl over two floors, its ragged end over the main entrance to the building, with bits of torn thread fluttering like streamers.

The boy's childish adulation for a great victory of the people was discovered a few minutes later, aided by the fact that, after unfurling the flag, he screamed 'Liberdade' so loudly it startled early coffee-drinkers at Casa Portugal around the corner, intent in a conservative bastion of Salcette taluka to do nothing more than spend another unhurried day in this civilized jewel among the colonies as the world outside continued to self-destruct. It brought swift reaction and retribution from Father Ivo, who, forgetting his vows of good behaviour and piety, brought down the rod of judgement, made of the best Malaccan cane, swiftly and repeatedly on the buttocks of the young fool who had dared mix the godly and ungodly and voice unthinkable thoughts such as power to the people—at his school, of all places. As he later told his fraternity, when he punished Olimpio for offending God and Portugal—not necessarily in that order—he was punishing himself, hoi. When he tenderly touched young Olimpio's lacerated and bloodied bums—this part he kept to himself, knowing most of his brothers would not commiserate—he was washing his hands in his own blood, may God forgive him.

Olimpio couldn't sit properly for nearly a week and, as he healed, the boy decided he would not let the unsavoury episode at school distract him from paying homage to his heroes, the makers of the new world at Yalta. Terrified of what his administrator father would think of his bringing home books and such on Allied heroes, Olimpio decided he would honour these stars in a way nobody would be able to prevent: when the time came, he would name his sons after them.

Olimpio despaired for three births, as Fatima Luisa appeared stubbornly set to produce three daughters—the stocky Guilhermina, the stick-thin Filomena and the surprising Pilomena. Just as all seemed lost, she brought forth Winston—named with much satisfaction after the wartime charioteer of Great Britain—a year after Portugal reluctantly gave up Aparanta to India. Rapidly over the next three years, other Allied war leaders were similarly enshrined: Franklin, the avenger of Pearl Harbour, and Iosif, named after a 'true hero' because, as Olimpio declared at the christening, in front of a nervous audience of family and neighbours, 'millions of lives and all are nutting-only when it comes to the mudderland, no?'

Fatima Luisa had willed herself to remain quiet while Olimpio ranted, her tired body refusing to give him any more heroes, a decision she blessed herself for in later years, when young Winston, a graduate of Olimpio's alma mater, showed signs of taking his legacy seriously. The boy slowly and surely read everything Churchill had ever spoken or written, although he eventually retained only the essence, not the English. He even spent his first profits—from assisting a local moneylender with a minor land-grab—to buy all twelve paperback volumes of Churchill's memoirs of World War II. He discovered these in a sidewalk bookstore at Flora Fountain during a celebratory whoring trip to Bombay with his fellow fledgling thugs, brothers Iosif and Franklin. Iosif had already assumed a dearer place in Winston's heart than Franklin on account of greater bravery: he did not blink when breaking a skull, knee or femur, or snapping the wrist of the nearly-with-the-Lord Father Ivo when he stupidly tried to revisit the sins he had committed with their father. Franklin, Winston considered a bit of a thinker and, therefore, a fop.

For their part, the brothers, less erudite than Winston and not as consumed as him with a sense of history and the future, were from the early years content to follow their leader-brother, relieved to let him take key decisions. Of course, such leadership was reinforced in their childhood in the form of severe beatings if they ever questioned him, but such piffle has never come in the way of destiny. Winston wanted to shape Aparanta in his own vision, marching along one emphatic step at a time. Money, power, money, power. 'Like army only, no?' he had preached to Iosif and Franklin soon after forcing the neighbourhood ice-cream vendor to part with his wares, free, of course. That had been near the church at Varca one Sunday evening the year Winston decided extortion would be a better course of study than pursuing college in Margao or Mapusa like a weakling. 'Lefts, rights, lefts, rights,' the already hulking thug-to-be had marched up and down the street, as his brothers applauded. 'Moneys, strengths, moneys, strengths,' Winston chanted cleverly in cadence, and Iosif and Franklin felt blessed. The brothers could see passers-by give them a wide berth and took heart from what fear could achieve.

Olimpio passed away soon after Winston had won his first election as the youngest-ever sarpanch of Varca in a stunning display of naked power. He introduced to Aparanta the concept of intimidating candidates by breaking their bones or burning their homes, and the insistent display of motorcades carrying unemployed youngsters and petty thugs glowering at prospective voters, while Winston, the star, held up a two-fingered victory sign with a huge smile.

At the church service for Olimpio's passing, Winston had inadvertently shamed Fatima Luisa to the core of her tired shell. With heartfelt kindness, he told her in front of guests, his voice soothing the microphone, 'Be strongs, no, mummy? KBO.' Just like his namesake, Winston imagined, would have exhorted his colleagues in the war cabinet as that funny-moustached Adolf, with less than quarter the moustache of the other Iosif, set about breaking prized masonry and people with his bombs and rockets and ideas.

Iosif, wearing a black bandana across his shaved head in keeping with the solemnity of the moment, smiled delightedly at his leader-brother's brilliance. Showing the gold in his teeth, he had leaned across to explain loudly into the microphone Winston's mysterious suggestion. 'Keep buggering on, no?' Then, completely missing the image of Fatima Louisa shrivelling into her black shroud, he had turned worshipfully to Winston and given him a thumbs-up of appreciation. 'Sol-*lid*, brudder.'

Winston, quick to recognize the bewildered expressions on the faces of his guests as something less than total approval, had graciously waved his jewelled fingers at Iosif, smiling his benevolent smile for his subjects while brewing anger so overpowering he began to blink. His eyes first became moist and then turned blood-red, a mysterious affliction that would from then on accompany Winston at times of great stress. But Winston controlled his seething well. Instead of instantly killing Iosif in front of everyone and completing two wakes at the cost of one, as his cunning brain urged him to do, he restricted himself to a vicious and faintly audible 'Bluddy id-*jut*.'

7. And Casa Serena Goes One Into Two

It is not what it once was, Casa Serena, the pride of Sodomo. Melba took care of that when she claimed half the mansion after Francesco went for his long walk with the Lord. She had brought the sarpanch—or bought, one never knew these days—that greedy son of a pig Janardan Naik, forever running after foreign women.

Naik had even tried that at Happy Bar one evening three seasons ago with Elke from Freiburg.

'No frien' you have?' he had stridently enquired. 'I am Johnny Naik, boss of Sodomo, no? I show you nice time.'

He had got upset with Tony when Elke, single and severe, had called him 'wichser' and emptied her bottle of beer on his head with a jangle of silver and coloured-stone bracelets.

'You calling me weak?' Janardan Naik had thundered. 'You know who I am? I am boss of Sodomo.'

'World famous in Sodomo,' Oldman Bob had said genially from his usual spot at one end of the bar, back against the wall, glass of dark rum and water within easy reach on the bar top, to his right. 'She said you're a wanker, mate.'

'*How* you know?' Janardan Naik was livid, and turned on Bob in his anger.

'I dropped by those parts for a few months in 1945 when I thought I was too young to get some but not too young to kill, but you wouldn't know much about that, would you?' He considered Johnny for a few seconds before he added, 'You'd best piss off before she lands the next bottle on your head.'

'*What* bitch-peoples you got, men?' Janardan Naik had demanded at the Villa's office as he helped himself to tissues from the intricately carved walnut-wood box on Tony's table to soak beer from his closely cropped head.

'Please don't do that again,' Tony said politely.

'What you mean?'

'Please don't come to the bar again. I have to ask you to leave now.'

'You God or *what,* men? You stop Johnny Naik, you or any bitch-peoples? You have problem next time and you see what Johnny Naik will do.'

Janardan Naik had kept his word. He had sat alongside the whore-bitch Melba, looking smug, while Melba smirked and Tony kept himself calm by breathing deeply.

The sarpanch began the preliminaries. 'Your mummy was your daddy's wife, so dis her house, no?'

'She is not my mother,' Tony had said evenly, as Melba and Janardan Naik grinned, and Tony briefly wondered if she had as generously gifted her plump body to the sarpanch as to her goats. 'This is not her house. I have lived here all my life. I have no idea where she came from.'

Tony thought he heard Anastasia giggle a little when he said this, but he was not sure. Melba's screech had drowned everything, and her body-hugging dress with padded shoulders, in Portuguese native-colonial fashion that had stopped in the 1950s as a speeding car would against a stone wall, billowed so threateningly that Tony was afraid her immense breasts might burst from their hold-all and spill on to the negotiating table. He had a brief vision of Janardan Naik attempting to retrieve them with great chivalry, but dismissed the thought to focus on the business at hand.

'But she was your daddy's wife, no?' Janardan Naik persisted.

'Perpet Saibinn will forgive her.'

'Sh-tup!' Melba shouted. 'Why you give bad-bad words? What dat old fool saw in you?'

'What did he see in *you*?'

'He see more woo-mans, more dan your mummy, no?'

If Anastasia were not by his side, and had not put a restraining hand on his arm, Tony swore later to Dino he would have snapped the armrests from the chair and driven one through Melba's heart and the other through Janardan Naik's, because he had only promised Francesco that he would behave at the funeral and was therefore not liable for anything that happened afterwards. This was afterwards, the Saibinn protect him.

Gabru had spoken up then in his role as mediator, trying to defuse the situation. 'No need for y'all to get angry. Why not talk like proper people and finish this as soon as possible? In Francesco's memory, no? Why give him trouble now?' He had made a sign of the cross, the same as when he suggested it was better to talk it over instead of going to court, for, in the manner of much law in the subcontinent, by the time judgement was passed only their spirits would be witness.

Things had settled after that. With Gabru's patient handling, they had worked out a settlement. Everyone agreed it would be best under the circumstances, especially as the usually punctilious Francesco had neglected to update his will after the death of Carmen and his surprising dalliance with Melba. Tony and Melba would split the twelve-room house down the middle, in the manner of some Hindu houses, behind the sprawling balcão. 'One into two, like chicken hot-sour soup, no?' Janardan Naik had offered with the élan of a gourmet.

They would divide the large living room and go straight as an arrow through the inner courtyard to the rear, cutting across the cavernous kitchen. It fell to Tony to re-equip it, as the cooking side with the old oven fell to Melba's territory, while his side had the well and most of the cupboards. They had agreed to share the well, as Anastasia said to fight over water would diminish what humanity there still remained, even though—the Saibinn knew—Melba had enough money for a new well and to fulfil the cost of dividing and re-equipping the house.

Now Melba had half the house, and also Tony's family name, which she grandly appended to hers, a conquest Tony could do nothing to reverse.

Everything on Tony's side, the room where he lived with Anastasia and everything on the walls and floors, belonged to Tony. Everything on the other side, including the master bedroom in which Melba rutted, was hers. (On some nights Melba and the goats caused such disturbance it seemed to Tony the rafters would descend to the floor in noisy protest, and all of Goa would break away from the Sahyadri Hills and slide into the Arabian Sea in aftershock and penitence. Consequently, Dino would also be rid of every manner of unhappiness, among them, MB, Russian drug lords and pimps, mining companies, land sharks, politicians, Father Gonsalves, PSI Fernandes, Winston and Number One—all because of an itinerant water buffalo in heat.) Melba had ordered one of her goats to try and move some furniture and porcelain from Tony's side of the living room in the middle of the night after negotiations for the partition had concluded, but Tony had wisely paid Umesh a hundred rupees as bonus to guard the room. Umesh had nearly taken off the goat's hand with a koito. His shouts had brought everyone into the room. When Tony turned on the lights—all switches were on his side of the room, the solution to that problem still days away—the tableau had revealed itself. The goat had his right hand clutched under his left armpit, wide-eyed, snarling with fear, ignorant of the stream of yellow urine on the mosaic floor creating channels as it nearly touched Umesh's feet. Umesh, chopper in upraised arm, eyes blazing, lips drawn back in fury, looked ready to kill, and Tony was struck by the similarity of the two expressions.

'Next time,' Umesh had offered in Konknni, in a calmer voice now with his patrao by his side, 'I will cut off your head and hang it from a coconut tree. If it feels lonely, I will cut off your cock and balls and put them around the neck so you have some friends to visit and a garland to wear at the same time.'

Melba, wearing a maxi-dress with loud tablecloth checks, managed a weak 'Sh-*tup*. Servant boy be servant boy' at Umesh's unexpected eloquence before pulling the shaken goat to his knees and dragging him into her bedroom.

Umesh had stayed in that room every night for fourteen days, as long as it took to partition and rewire the single-storeyed house, now mocking its given name of Casa Serena. But Melba did manage a small victory, when she persuaded a hapless goat to trot across the back and uproot the green chilli trees in the kitchen garden. The theft made Conceição the cook fret for a few days until Tony got hold of some saplings from their neighbour Vinay Kamat, who had been an occasional drinking partner to Francesco and his casual adviser in tax matters.

Soon, a second letterbox went up on Melba's side of the house: Melba Rodrigues de Sousa. Tony made sure to tell Mahesh Parab, the postman, of the development before a letter meant for Anastasia or him went erroneously to Melba and disappeared forever.

So, in a manner, Melba laid claim to Casa Serena. But Tony clearly told her to leave Villa de Vida alone, or he would show her what hell really looked like.

'Zollo,' Melba hissed, but quickly left the house with some goat called Edmund, or was it Agnel or Princewell.

'Chedi,' Tony had viciously muttered in revenge, also in Konknni, but Melba had already swept off, so only the wind and Conceição heard Melba and Antonio. The withered cook made a sign of the cross over her heart, not knowing which would invite the Saibinn's ire more: Melba calling Antonio a cockroach and going off with one of her young lovers on a motorcycle, Francesco not even properly settled in his modest tomb, or Tony in turn calling her a whore-bitch—a prize one at that.

Anastasia absorbed all this, the same as she had absorbed everything from the day her name changed from Gracias to Sousa, this delicate doctor's daughter, 'her features so fine you don't have to see her papers, you can see she is descendente', Carmen had preened, ever mindful of the primacy of Portuguese stock in Aparanta. Ida, typically, had dismissed it. 'There you go again,' she had snapped, 'as if there is any way to tell who really is a descendente and who a mestiço any more, we're all so mixed up. It doesn't matter, she is a lovely girl and I would take her as my own even if she were a fisherman's daughter. Carmen, you really cannot forget the old days, no?'

Tony had overheard this as he unexpectedly walked into the room from the Villa. Francesco had been parking the old Peugeot in the driveway of Casa Serena, reversed so it would be easy to take out to reach Ida home. Dinner was just over and Anastasia was in the kitchen bringing out a bowl of her divine serradura, powder-fine biscuit covering a mousse. Carmen had had the grace to look a little shamefaced, as Ida beamed at Tony, as if being with Anastasia was the grandest act in his life. And it had been.

Long after Tony and Anastasia had taken their vows in front of a tortured Christ, a large part of Sodomo and Saligao, and what seemed like all of Anastasia's clan from Raia from Salcette taluka, they had stood whispering to each other. 'I will be with you till the end of your days,' Tony had told her in a suddenly strong voice, surprising himself as much as Anastasia and those who could hear his passion from the front pews. 'Me too,' Anastasia had replied without fuss, and glowed as amber. She had smiled at him, their sights locking in complete belief in the afterlife of marriage.

Such foolishness, Tony thinks. Now the days never end. He looks at Anastasia as her slender form busies itself in the kitchen, and the smell of fresh lemon juice and chopped green chilli wafts towards him. And onions. There are always onions these days as there are always tears.

Tony knows, as Conceição had told him one day, about how, too proud to show grief to the world, Anastasia hid her sorrow by refusing to let Conceição or anyone else touch the onions because that would take away her tears. How could she hold so much tear water, Tony wonders. We should call her Anastasia of the Waters, Patron Saint of Miserable Creatures.

He stops himself, ashamed of his rage. Things would need to turn soon, or they would both go insane with sourness.

8. Aperitif for the Innkeeper

'How was your day?' Anastasia asks. Her face is streaked with tears. She looks at Tony, unapologetic and defiant, glorious in grief.

'Okay. Some trouble at the Villa. Some problem guests, nothing new.' Tony is wary. 'How are you?'

'Does it matter?'

'Why shouldn't it matter?' Tony knows this is how the end begins. When marriage begins to blister and peel like paint from walls during the wet, churlishness is a sign of companionship. Anastasia turns back to the chopping board. The beat of the large kitchen knife against wood is furious and liquid with its passage through layers of onion.

Tony cannot control his irritation. 'How much onion do you want us to eat? These days I sweat onions. There's so much sulphur inside me I must be careful to walk in the shade. You want to cry, you cry. Why do you need onions to cry? Why must we all drown because you won't come out of your well?'

Loud reggae music can be heard through the wall, past the rafters, and it tears into him, urging him to get up, stand up, fight for his rights.

'Shut up,' Tony roars, and is instantly contrite. Anastasia has given a little scream of fright.

Evidently, a goat is listening, and the volume is turned down enough so they can hear themselves clearly. Tony's headache recedes—he doesn't recall when it began. He pours a glass of water and absently sips from it. Anastasia, also calmer, steps into the interlude.

'You are not the same since Francesco died.'

'What do you expect me to say?'

'You are not like this at the Villa.'

'That's a fucking circus. I have to smile for guests.'

'And here?' Anastasia is mellow, inviting.

'It is like hell here with that whore-bitch,' Tony exhales. 'I hope she dies. Shit-fuck-bitch!' He is mildly surprised that he can these days curse with the ease of Dino.

'We could sell this place, Tony. We can't let others poison us, no? Why can't we take a room at the Villa till we find a proper place? Keep household things with Aunty Ida or Mummy and Daddy? They won't mind, no?' Anastasia raises her voice. 'They worry about you.'

'This is my home.' Tony dismisses the suggestion with a wave of his hand, realizing too late that Anastasia hates the gesture, to her it's more insulting than a rude word. 'How can you understand what it is like for me?'

'I don't understand you any more.' There is the abyss, again.

And Tony plunges. 'Did you? Did you ever?'

They are placed on hold by the ringing of a mobile phone. In his distress Tony searches for the phone inside his pockets, before, drawn by its blue light, he realizes it hangs from a cord around his neck. Anastasia is smiling, and for an exquisite moment they recognize each other. Then he takes the call and the moment is gone, although Anastasia will not let it pass without battle and continues to gaze at him in her assured, unblinking way—searing or soothing, Tony has always found difficult to gauge.

It's the Professor, breathless, all pretence at lyricism gone. Florian and Rainer, the gay German couple, are arguing loudly at the bar and have even slapped each other, and guests are complaining. 'And Mark got Sally a drink and that long-haired Israeli girlfriend of his walked in—Yell...Yellow...God knows *what*, men—she walked in just as they said cheers with arms linked and she came and pushed both of them and started shouting, all fuck-fuck, dis-dat. That girl from Delhi, no? She told the Israeli girl to go back to the gutter she came from. So she said, "Fuck off Indian bitch" and went off and all. She took her bags and went off with some boy who was outside on a bike, you know those old Bullets painted with hippie-type colours, all flower…floro…*fuck,* men, all shiny in the dark and all. Who will pay the bill, men? That Mark, money he has or what? Are you sleeping, patrao? Can you come for two minutes? And Dino is here, asking if you are coming? If you don't come soon I don't know *what* will happen…'

'Professor? Ay, Professor? Calm down. I'll be there soon. Okay?'

Tony disconnects, and gently rubs his forehead with thumb and forefinger. For a heartbeat, Anastasia's eyes soften and she wants to rush to him. But the temptation passes as she blinks. She stays by the onions.

'Oh Perpet!' Tony moans, his eyes on the floor, missing both Anastasia's cue and retraction. 'Shit-shit-shit.'

'I miss Maria,' Anastasia says after a while, looking up from her plaint-board at Tony, seated at the small round table in the kitchen covered in a cloth showing a view of Cologne, a gift from Florian-Rainer. A half-empty glass of water is in front of him, and he idly turns it between his palms.

'Sometimes I dream of her.'

'I have to go now.' Tony is gentle, tired.

Anastasia doesn't hear Tony. 'I wake up and I am cold. It's like the wind is bringing in her spirit to be warmed. So young, no? So helpless.'

'Don't blame yourself,' Tony says, his heart dissolved, glad for the alibi the onions provide. 'Who is to blame?'

But Anastasia isn't looking at him. Her delicate skin is stretched tight over the achingly beautiful face that Tony still craves but can't bring himself to touch, and it hurts him more than the sorrow they both try to pretend doesn't exist. Anastasia is crossing the river tonight, and there is truth on the other side. 'Maria brought belief back into our lives. Our love can't make us forget that we are not together any more, Tony. What we have is not together.'

She looks at him, and to Tony it is like a knife, because her eyes can melt and kill at once. It's a special gift she has, a gift he has worshipped since he first met her at the carnival, where he was yelling and waving his hat at the girls on the floats like a damn fool, drunk along with his friends on cheap whisky and feeling joy he did not want to control. And there, outside Bar Manuel, standing on a red plastic chair was a vision he hadn't seen before. This girl laughing at him, the setting sun creating a halo around her head in the haze of his drink—though not enough for him to ignore her dancing eyes and the straight hair that played about her face.

If he wasn't beset with alcohol he would never have done it, walking up to her and bowing like some grandee from the old days and asking, 'May I have this dance?' She had stepped down from the chair, and they had danced right there, swaying to music from bands that sometimes preceded a float or were placed on one, changing their rhythm with every change in song. They danced in front of a surprised crowd—because people from good families did not show emotion in public except the occasional smile of indulgence; they merely stood with wooden faces as joy and the lower classes went by.

'There cannot be anyone else in my life but you,' Anastasia is saying in Konknni, in the more lilting tones and fluid words of the south. 'Why are we like this, Tony?'

Tony knows that she speaks the truth. With her, it's a home, even with the whore-bitch living a wall away. Anastasia and he are both destitute. The unborn Maria could have made them whole, he imagines. But she wouldn't wake, wouldn't scream her welcome to the world, and wouldn't clench her fists in anger at not finding someone to hold her close, a comforting breast, the awkward but loving cradle of a father's arm. She had lain there on the table on a rough white hospital towel, beautiful like her mother, but silent and blue, and Anastasia and Tony had known that their togetherness would have to search for another reason.

'It is not your fault,' Tony is saying. 'How can any mother wish her child dead?' He regrets saying it as soon as he does, because Anastasia flinches as if he has slapped her, and turns away.

Melba had said as much, shouting across the balcão as Tony helped Anastasia from the back seat of the car when she returned home from her father's nursing home in Margao, Benedito Gracias, deliverer of hundreds—including Anastasia—unable to do anything for his granddaughter except wring his hands and curse God for not inviting him ahead of the baby.

Typically, Melba had ensured Tony was also caught in the web. 'He has demon seed, no?' She had announced to the world: the families Sousa, Gracias and an impressive clot of Sodomo. 'How anyting will grow with poison? Now you are finish, no more baby-baby, You say sorry to God, but what about his demon seed and your poisoned field? What you do now? Put fertilizer only?'

Before she could go on, Conceição, who had been watching from the bottom of the partitioned stairs, had screeched something unintelligible, stormed up the steps on Melba's side and slapped her face to shut the filth. Anastasia's mother had looked ready to repeat what Conceição had done, and even Francesco's stoicism had broken to fix his second wife with a look of pure hatred. Tony would later wonder if that was the day Francesco had finally decided it was time to leave.

After a week of silent grieving Tony had escaped to the Villa, and thereafter his days there had only grown longer. The onions had gathered strength soon after Anastasia gathered the will to stand, and after her mother had left for home with the plea, 'Look after my child, Tony.'

There is now nothing for Tony to tell Anastasia. It is not the right time to talk of the innocence of perpetual commitment or the agonizing foolishness of pure love. He knows of nothing else that lives and dies at the same time, as love does; it leaves no indication of passing till it presumes resurrection. It hurts that we cannot forget Maria, Tony mourns. It hurts that we cannot mend ourselves. His heart breaks when Anastasia impales herself on him, going through the motions of love and longing, crying even as she desperately tries to please them both, punishing herself as she punishes him for all the broken glass in their heaven.

'Dear God,' he whispers to the wind, fumbling for the ignition, his head bowed over the steering wheel of his dented, comforting grey jeep. 'I never thought love could be so cruel.'

9. The Life and Times of Winston Almeida: II

Over the years, Winston Almeida displayed great facility for doing on land what his hunter-gatherer cousins, blindingly swift and colossally shrewd, did in water. He too came stealthily upon his prey to devour in sometimes ungainly but always emphatic bites.

Only, Winston never advertised his intention with cavalier flash of dorsal fin and grotesque display of teeth. In that, he was cleverer than his cousins, some of whom occasionally landed at his table, their tough hides flayed, white flesh with a strong taste of the sea first filleted and then blanched with vinegar, red chilli and a score of spices. Lumena, his wife, ensured there was black pepper too, and Winston liked it for the same reason that the conquistador and great trading houses of Europe had. Pepper made for fruits of the sea or heavy meats on board great ships and on the great tables of Europe to be better preserved, more palatable and, during the stately journey through the innards of sailors and society, also made it easier to pass wind. According to Winston, his mother made better shark ambot-tik than Lumena. It was a judgement Lumena was wise not to contest, since the only time she had offered comment of any kind, that too publicly, she had been scarred by a shake of Winston's fin.

At the fest of the church at Varca, a large knot had collected around the Almeidas, already gathering road-kill legend with a number of awe-inspiring real estate deals. (After all, hadn't Winston given a week's time to the widow Paciencia Sequeira to sign the deed of her vast beachfront property in Benaulim? A full week before her son, the strapping Luis, was found by the tracks near Dudh Sagar

Station far to the east, spray from the imposing waterfall washing his body mysteriously missing a set of legs below the knees, the same legs with which Luis scored goals with such panache at parish football tournaments to which Winston was a most generous benefactor. And wasn't Dulceta Figueiredo blessed with Winston's seed, now grown into a robust and confused boy, because her father Basil was foolish enough to refuse a matchless offer to sell his sprawling hundred-year-old house in Margao, which stood in the way of Winston's large office-and-shopping complex in the borderlands of the old and new cities?) It had been magical, like the walkabouts of his namesake during the Battle of Britain. A convoy of tooting scooters and motorcycles carried Winston's henchmen, as Winston acknowledged the cheers of the crowd with a small wave of jewelled hands, smiling the smile of a modest man.

Into this general glow of adulation had stepped the hapless Lumena, daring to humiliate Winston in front of his subjects. It was a small matter, such as it was. White-haired Engineer Agnelo had asked if it wasn't time the spinster Pilu, Winston's favourite sister, got married with the grace of God and the generosity of Babush Santana, a widower saxophonist and acknowledged performer at reputed night clubs across Calcutta, Madras and fancy hotels by the Mandovi. A middle-aged but good man, perfect for the still pretty and plump-as-fresh-sannas, Pilu. Plump sannas and spicy sorpatel made for a blessed pairing, Engineer Agnelo had said, and onlookers laughed to acknowledge his naughty wit. To Winston's query whether Babush was a GOL—which the ever-present Iosif had graciously explained to the gathering as 'Gentleman of Leisure, no?'—Engineer Agnelo had agreed, Yes, Babush was indeed a GOL in the best tradition of Nova Goa, having leveraged his savings into becoming a minor moneylender and then a minor property dealer. Winston understood that well: a forfeited loan was always an opportunity to build assets.

'He's from Ilhas,' Engineer Agnelo had gently continued, using the preferred colonial term for Tiswadi taluka, his tone an apology for introducing a southerner's sister to a northerner. 'But that's okay, no?'

Lumena, who until then few had suspected of possessing a sense of humour as sharp as her husband's business dealings, had in defence of Pilu broken through her cowed demeanour to exclaim, 'Why, no? Sogllem fuloit mortam.' This led to shocked intakes of breath as well as a few titters, as the double entendre of this Konknni saying, 'we all die blowing', was delicious in delivery and irony. Winston had instantly gone red in the eyes and not caring about his blurred vision had turned around and unerringly slapped Lumena across her face, instinct telling him she would be right where he expected her to be, three paces behind, a little to the left, her face conveniently in the course of his arm when it was raised and parallel to the ground. The contact was hard enough for her lips to be cut, for blood to run down the corner of her mouth, finding courses in the now cracked pancake of the heavy foundation on her face, a veil to mask from the world the other points of contact.

Lumena had smiled apologetically, but Winston, who was by then blinking so rapidly and hard that his face appeared to be twitching, had stormed to his car and driven away. That left Lumena to walk through the village, back to the large, grey-coated, open-faced brick house with immense columns and Lego triangles built by the best masons of Margao, Winston's honour to his hero's birthplace home, Blenheim Palace.

Winston had taken photographs of the building on a week-long pilgrimage of Great Britain by way of Fernandes Bros & Fly Tours & Travels of Margao, immediately after consummating his deal with Figueiredo & Fly. It had been a tour marred by disaster, as the Duke of Marlborough declined to shake Winston's hand and guards wouldn't let him enter either 10 Downing Street or the Admiralty.

But it had not shaken Winston's faith in his pug-faced hero or the nation he had defended. Indeed, Winston's admiration for Britain was further enhanced by an old-fashioned British sandwich offered by two girls—one Swedish, the other West Indian—after a tip offered by Atanásio, the first Fernandes of Fernandes Bros & Fly, that Winston must visit a telephone booth. 'Brudder,' Atanásio had exclaimed, 'what putting, no, making appointment from phone-boot wit visiting card stuck in boot! Card only will give organism. Great country, boss!' And Winston had to agree.

After that day, Lumena had not spoken a word to Winston unless asked to, suffering beatings in silence, opening her plump thighs to accommodate Winston's half-minute bursts of domination and infinitesimal spurt of sperm. But after Tojo, Tito and Tarzan, before another T could arrive, Lumena had quietly, with complicity of the doughty Pilu, visited a well-known gynaecologist in Margao who provided discreet aid to women in distress, to have her tubes severed. Lumena and Pilu covered well their moral distress, hoping that Jesus, His Mummy—a strong woman by all accounts—His Daddy and Their Church would surely understand and forgive Lumena this trespass to limit descendants of Winston, so reducing the chances of another one turning out like the father. (To reinforce her mission, Lumena also vowed to ensure her sons did not evolve as their father had, but this promise she kept strictly to herself.)

◆

And so, to the conqueror's march. In the manner unbridled piracy in business is often transformed into respectable legitimacy in a few short years, Winston Almeida continued to prosper. He breathed into a brand of give-and-take impetus so profound that practitioners of gentility had no antidote except to hope their lives and land would not lie on the map this feasting man had drawn. And, as with many good men of present-day Aparanta who must claim their place in history, Winston one day decided at a peremptory meeting with his brothers at the now too-small six-bedroom house they shared that he would like to own a football club.

'What peoples in Goa love?' he asked rhetorically early one Sunday evening, after he had done his putting with Lumena.

He guessed Iosif had put Carla, because the fool had a smile on his face that would not come off. '*How* bugger can enjoy putting with wife too much?' briefly entered Winston's head as a thought before he batted away craven sentimentality as he would a pestering dragonfly. But Franklin, who for all his naming after an American president was both unmarried and unaffected—'If for putting only why to get married?' he had once asked with complete sincerity and Winston had seen wisdom in that thought—mistook Winston's query as meriting an answer.

'Fish curry and rice,' Franklin said, eagerly.

'Id-*jut*,' Winston thundered. 'Dat like blood to we Goan peoples, no? But what you love like putting only?'

This time Franklin wisely kept quiet, allowing Winston to finish the thought, as a true leader should. 'Football, no?'

'Aaaanh,' Iosif and Franklin had intoned. They realized instinctively, in the manner of a band of brothers entwined in the peculiarly coded double-helix of Olimpio and Fatima Luisa, that something truly impressive was on its way.

'What-appened, no, what all we do in Goa we are still son-of-a-schoolmaster.' Winston's dismissive tone made it a curse. 'Dis big house, all dese places we are owning, nutting for dese old families and all. You see dem, no, sitting on balcão in Altinho with all dat lace-lace curtains, same like peoples in Aldona, Verna, Loutolim, Raia, nort, sout, dis-dat, sitting all day, like dey all owns perfume company and when dey are doing fuski, dey tink perfume only is coming from bum. But dat perfume is used by fodrechea mens, all real mens use Brut. So like dat we need to do big-people tings.'

He dug out a stubborn shred of oyster from his teeth with a finger and flicked it away, past Franklin's ducking head. A small army of red ants mysteriously appeared to carry away their trophy. Winston looked around for effect, because what he would say next required a stage of gravity.

'Football is respect, and respect is football.' He blinked. 'What you tink? I make football team, no? Den all dis old family peoples will kiss my bum. Bugger what dey put under armpit. *What* matters?'

'*What* matters,' agreed Iosif. 'What you call team, boss?'

That pleased Winston, for in that moment he knew he had earned true admiration from his family, his place in the hierarchy secure for all time. 'Almeida United, no? Like Manchester and all. How it sounds?'

'Sol-*lid*, brudder,' Iosif was ecstatic. Franklin, already struck with a premonition of fame, remained smilingly silent.

Then Winston outlined the design for the club flag and jersey. It would be split vertically in fluorescent green ('Dis richful cover of mudder eart'), red ('Eart of Goa only') and blue ('Like sea, no?'). At the centre of the red slash there would be a deeper red-and-white football. And so the grand enterprise was formed.

Fuelled by Aparanta's limitless talent that thrived in every vaddo of every near and far-flung village and nurtured in the grounds of every municipality, Almeida United took wing. Each year it steadily moved up, from the ranks of village tournaments to the taluka. Finally, just a dizzying four years after it was formed, Almeida United was rechristened Al U by the adoring public of Varca and entire Salcette taluka after it gained a place in Aparanta's premiership. The club earned respect even in areas north of the Zuari River—a chasm claimed to be as great as the global north-south divide, or at least the 'Catlick-Indu' divide by some among Aparanta's intelligentsia. At any rate, Almeida United earned a place as contender among

Aparanta's biggest clubs.

Winston's rules were simple in the manner a shark might lull a dolphin into believing it had no interest in the puny human floundering in the border of shallow and deep, only to pounce once the dolphin, resplendent in delusion, had disappeared after playfully planting a kiss on the human's nose.

He followed utmost professionalism at Al U, taking care of his players, never once breaking the legs of a centre forward or a left or right winger if he missed a goal, or the hands of the goalkeeper if he let one in, or feed the boy-child of the opposing team's star player to crabs even if he scored the winning goal against his team. Iosif and Franklin urged him often enough, and Winston too wished it, but he knew he would cross that bridge if he ever came to it. Meanwhile, he took out his disappointment in other ways. A slap or two to Lumena; taking Tojo's head and playfully hitting it against a wall; or going to the cemetery at night to urinate on the gravestone of former panchayat member Arvind Colaco—among a silly few who would not be coerced by Winston into signing papers to fraudulently convert village land, farm or forest for commercial use for one of Winston's apartment houses or shops.

Self-control with football players added a winning gloss to Winston's respectability, as he had known it would. He didn't have to build great industry or schools—that could come later, if needed. All he required to gather public sympathy was give the people football, and now and again sponsor the church fest. Meanwhile, he could loot, rape and pillage in the glorious tradition of Aparanta and, alongside, ensure Al U won a few tricky matches with the impressive talent of his players enhanced by creative spontaneity of the referee—purchased outright with a handsome payment of rupees and the grand arts of coercion perfected by Iosif. For those who were steadfast in their support and performance for Al U, there were shopping-and-putting trips to Bombay and Bangalore complete with banknotes to throw at dancing girls.

By diligently pursuing his goal, Winston built a reputation that soon spread far beyond Salcette. Old businesses grudgingly began to acknowledge him. Community leaders looked to his support to win elections. Principals of schools flocked to him to be guest of honour at a singing competition or an art exhibition. 'Be strong, no?' he would urge little children. '*What* matters what peoples say? Be strong only.' If they didn't love him, many enthusiastically applauded him. Even successive Number Ones took note of Goa's newest bandit—and, hence, possible ally—on the make.

It was at this time that Winston took to wearing all-white clothes, down to underwear and socks, by day, and all-black clothes, underwear and socks included, after nightfall. He brokered a truce when it came to shoes—two-toned, imported from Madras—to add a rakish streak to the ensemble. He briefly toyed with the idea of taking to cigars, but unlike the First Sea Lord he could not establish a reliable channel for the supply of Romeo y Julieta. He gave up on it for good after a minion visited Bombay and mistakenly brought back a copy of a play about doomed lovers by someone called William Shakespeare. This led Winston, after the ritual rapid blinking and eyes turning crimson, to push the book down the throat of the hapless underling. And he, barely into the ranks with tight T-shirt, slim moustache, fat gold chain and big motorbike, was permanently cured of tonsillitis.

10. A Crowd and the Innkeeper's Cross

Peace is restored in the Villa by the time Tony arrives. Rainer and Florian are mended and are getting drunk on cheap Indian brandy.

'Tony my gut friend,' Florian reaches out to grab his hand, 'Vee are now making gut holiday, ja? Like gut boys, ja?'

Tony smiles. Rainer has reached across the bar top to grab the spout of the soda dispenser, which has Wonderbar written on it. He scrutinizes it, seems to make up his mind, holds it up like a microphone and loudly begins to sing over and over in a rich tenor, *'Das ist wunderbar…'* Florian looks at him with affection and turns his head around to show Rainer off to other guests, as some good-naturedly applaud Rainer's slurred effort.

Mark, evidently recovered from the encounter with the infuriated, banyan-haired Yael, is now explaining karma to Sally. 'Give up peace and go for killing? What was I thinking? Silicon Valley to Death Valley, for the cause of universal peace? I'm like, Jesus!' His left hand holds Sally's right across the small cane table, managing to find space between the stand with half a candle and the bowl of roasted peanuts, three empty bottles of beer for him and two empty glasses of Mon Soon for Sally. She is on her third robust drink: the Mon Soon brings with it three fingers of dark rum, mixed with a moderate lashing of ginger lemonade and topped with a storm of cold beer and mint sprigs to taste. Mark lazily strokes her tanned cheek. 'Karma will kick you in the butt each time, you know?' he continues. Tony will swear Sally is purring, but the noise in the bar hides her expression of pleasure. Instead, the world sees her rapt face.

Oldman Bob is there at his usual place at the end of the bar. He sits with his back to the wall, smiling at the world over his glass of lager, Panama hat tipped low. Bob grins as Tony makes his way through the throng that sways unselfconsciously to Buddy Guy's singing over the house system he has the blues, from his head down to his shoes.

In the near corner, framed by elderly mirrors that advertise Franziskaner Weissbier from Bavaria and Amstel Light, is a small group of Russian royalty. The men wear knitted shirts, blue jeans and snakeskin boots that set off their cowboy-style hats. The three women with them are young, astoundingly pretty and laden with glittering rocks. Two wear low-slung jeans with the edges of their jewelled undergarments showing above the waistbands, the third wears a nearly non-existent skirt. The royals exude danger like an animal trap. This evening, there are none who wish to go searching for their heads at the bottom of the Mandovi, or the Chapora to its north, for so it is rumoured happens to silly folk who presume to either challenge the empire of the new Tsars or usurp their harem.

'Shit,' Tony thinks, stretching his lips in a smile.

Sergei Yurlov sees Tony and lazily waves, holding up a bottle of Indian sparkling wine. It is all Happy Bar serves and they are polite not to bring their own Cristal or Dom Perignon, as they are known to do at other establishments, insisting they have the right to drink what they want, where they want. The Villa does this to people. Maybe the Saibinn, whom Francesco appealed to for blessings when they broke ground for the Villa, has woven some special magic that brings people together from orbits that may otherwise never intersect before they continue on their particular ellipses. It prevents them from tearing through completely to another dimension, so wars are never consummated at the Villa or at Happy Bar, that grim work takes place elsewhere.

Tony waves back at Sergei, with a loud Tovarisch! Sergei roars his mirth and points an index finger at Tony, face improbably red. The cocked thumb goes up in a flourish of an imaginary shot. And I am a dead man, Tony thinks.

One of the girls, the one with the barely hidden jewel, turns to see where Sergei is pointing, and gives Tony a smile that he would return with equal warmth were it not for Sergei. Tony glimpses the profile of a perfect breast encased in a fur-lined bikini top. A little gold bell juts out of the brocade cup that holds her breast. Tony is certain when it is quieter he will be able to hear it. He inhales and turns his head in a slow arc towards Bob, who has been watching him.

'You got a regular zoo t'night, mate, an 'appy zoo. Good business at th' bar. Francesco would've been shocked, poor boy, but it's amazing 'ow the crowd's all changed in two-three years, innit? Settled down a bit now,' he says soothingly. 'For a while, the Professor looked like 'e'd 'ave a shit.'

Magically, the Professor appears next to Bob, comforted by familiar faces and unmindful of the gentle insult. Tony raises an eyebrow at Zezito, who discreetly shows three fingers and then glances at his watch. Tony manages a quick glance at his own, an old Omega Seamaster beloved of Francesco. It's not yet an hour since the licence to drink was delivered by phone at 8 p.m. by his beloved Magdalena and already the Professor is awash. It will be a long night.

Tony claps his hands on the Professor's shoulders and he almost chokes. '*What,* men?' Then he recovers. 'Mad people dis.'

'Take it easy, Prof. Dino here?'

'In your office, baba.' He takes a deep breath and looks at Tony. 'You're not angry I asked you to come, no?'

He is, but Tony has with him a commandment of Francesco: 'Never cut with a blunt knife because those wounds take longer to heal, and people then remember longer, no?' He puts his hand on the Professor's shoulder. 'What's the problem, chief? That bastard brother-in-law of yours asking for money again?'

'*Yes*, men,' the Professor says. 'But this time it's very bad. Minguel made me give him money to buy land for us near Tivim and now he says there is a problem with the title. Too many claimants. Lawyers, judges… I'm going crazy, men.'

'Where is the money?'

'Minguel took it-ré. He says he gave it to the seller and some to the panchayat people to make the paperwork easy, and now it is gone. How do I pay for the children's college and all?'

'Has he shown you the papers?'

'*What* papers, men?' The Professor whispers furiously. 'He says it is all gone. Money is with the seller, the papers are in court. I gave my brother-in-law cash, no? I have no receipt also.'

'Do you keep your head in your bum?'

Bob laughs at this and looks away, embarrassed to be caught eavesdropping.

'What to do, baba? My wife said, no? How I can say no?'

'Next time Magdu wants something, you tell her to ask her brother.'

'Simple teacher I was, no?' The Professor concedes defeat. 'Round and round—home to school to bar to home. Peaceful. Bas! Finish! How I bluddy got into all this shit-fuck things only the Saibinn knows.'

'Don't put it on her, boss,' Tony cautions wearily. 'She's doing overtime these days.'

Tony moves on, wading through his ocean, smiling at everybody and nobody. It's a busy mid-October night, and the world has gathered at Happy Bar. Shakuntala Singh waves in greeting.

'Tilly, all well? Forgotten Delhi already?' Tony jokes.

She smiles, thick eyebrows perfectly arched over kohl-lined eyes, seated at the other end of the bar from Bob, chatting with Terttu-Lüsa from Finland. Tilly raises her glass of vodka flooded with ice, a slice of lemon and two drops of Angostura bitters.

'It's the asshole I un-married I need to forget,' she answers Tony. 'Have you seen Dino around? He said he'd meet me here.'

Before he can reply, Terttu-Lüsa, glowing from a day of grilling her body in the sun and from the contents of the now empty shot glasses in front of her—enough tequila to numb a monitor lizard, Tony sees—leans across and gives Tilly a slow kiss on her cheek, briefly tapping her tongue on a mole. Tilly ignores the gesture and continues her conversation, but the Professor, who has seen it, flinches. Tony watches him shake his little finger like a twig in a storm, trying to catch Zezito's attention.

Tony is in conversation with himself behind the fixed smile: It's getting to the Professor. He is two people, and it is getting to him. These days we are all two people. We change our masks and lives with every hour so it is only natural we will sometimes forget who we really are. But who the fuck is counting and why the fuck am I speaking…thinking…speaking…like Dino?

11. Old Acquaintances and a Princess

It amazes Tony how music never kills conversation. It just drives some people to talk louder and talk more, even if they are drinking alcohol-free cocktails decorated with tiny, colourful parasols, bits of orange rind and canned cherries. Perhaps that is why, full of sugar, they chatter like wound-up toys till energy runs out. 'That is okay,' Tony says to himself. 'Ask, and you shall receive. You get your fill, and I get some money to keep alive Francesco's dream and decorate my empty life. Give, no? Bugger, *give*.'

Voices swirl around him, every table and group of people a whirlpool of conversation.

'I don't want to talk to them…'

'*Talk* to them, no? How it hurts you? You directly ship the ore to China instead of using middlemen and you bring something back.'

'What do I bring back?'

'You need some ballast, no? Load the ship with thermocol if you need to, ha-ha. Why to worry?'

Boys from Vasco.

'How're y'all, Mr Machado?' Tony tests the eddies. 'Long time. All well at home?'

'Ah, Tony, thanks, all is well. You don't seem to have place for us any more, with all your outsider guests. Good for business… good for Goa, I guess.' Pascoal Machado offers his joke. 'How is the beautiful Anastasia? Have you met Uday Kamat? My associate—he has just started a new shipping agency. U.K., this is Tony. His father Francesco—Frankie, no? How can I call my friend "Francesco"?—he built this place, and see what Tony has done with it. He has grown it without destroying the beauty.'

'Thanks, Mr Machado. Pleasure to meet you, Mr Kamat, welcome to Happy Bar. Y'all enjoy yourself. Zezito! Send some snacks over here. Some tisreo and chouriço. How y'all doing with your drinks?' The innkeeper has not deserted our Tony. 'Some wine for you, Mr Machado? We have a nice light red from Portugal.'

'Obrigado.'

'Não é nada.'

'Mr Kamat?'

'Johnny Black with soda, top-top. Thank you, thanks.'

'You're welcome,' says Tony by way of farewell. 'Excuse me.'

In the sit-out, he can hear Emily loudly calling someone a 'turd' and making it quite clear that if he doesn't put his shirt back on, she will call the police. That must be Joaozinho Mesquita, ready to open his shirt to any woman at Happy Bar after two beers and announce he receives eighty thousand rupees a month in pension from the Portuguese government, enough to philander with at will.

Emily is fighting back. 'I don't care if you've taken a piss with Christopher fucking Columbus or Valentino da Gama...'

Let them sort it out, Tony tells himself. I'm needed only for real war. He turns, and freezes in shock when he notices the guests at the corner table near the entrance. He cannot believe his eyes would betray him, for he has not noticed sooner: PSI Fernandes.

His companion is a tall lady, even seated she is a head taller than Fernandes. Her dress, patterned with bright orange and yellow flowers, is cut low in front, her large breasts highlighted by straight hair that cascades around her. She turns to look towards him, slowly twisting her body. Heavy-lidded eyes settle on him and she smiles. Tony catches a flash of gold in her teeth. *Mãe de Deus!* He walks towards their table, anxious to find out what PSI Fernandes is doing here with the Amazon. Amazon, right? Dino will know, Dino always knows the right words.

'Caetano, darling,' she asks PSI Fernandes in a heavy voice, 'a friend of yours?'

Tony sees a flash like a windscreen wiper moving across her eyes every second or so, and wonders briefly if he has lost his mind, until he realizes it's the lazily turning blades of the antique fan playing off her irises. Blue shadow on the lids and glitter in the corner of her eyes. The effect, highlighted by her smooth, light-cafe skin, is mesmerizing.

The lady pronounces Caetano correctly in the Portuguese way, swallowing the last vowel in the word. But it's more lilting when she says it.

Caetano, never thought his name is Caetano. Alex, even a Joseph, but not Caetano. Can a pig-fucker be Caetano and do susu on a saint's name? Tony is in a whirlpool.

'Ay, Fernandes, what are you doing here?'

Fernandes turns around and flinches at seeing Tony, and Tony's head silently screams curses. Whoreson, thief, didn't you know this is my place? Tony is nearly blind with rage. Why the surprise? Or are you here, showing up after all these years because pig-fuckers always bring pig-fucking bad news? What does the Saibinn charge these days? Two candles for one curse? Or is she greedier about equal-to? Is this about Dino?

'Ah, Tony Calangute, is it?' Fernandes recovers and straightens to full height. 'Fernandes, is it? Police Inspector Fernandes, Tony Calangute,' he declares with a smile. 'PI, more than PSI. Un'stan'?' Fernandes is eager to save face. 'So, dis now your place?' He waves his left arm, and Tony sees a gold watch. The button of Fernandes's silk batik shirt is open and Tony can see a thick gold chain amid a mass of hair. The top of a gold pen clipped to the pocket glitters even in the dim light of the bar. The cologne is so strong the mosquitoes will surely keep away from this table, no need for frankincense in burning coir, or coils of mosquito repellent that leave neat curving bits of ash-turd as they burn. Not bad, Fernandes, Tony breathes in; you must be a busy man, you bastard.

'Yes. I thought you knew,' he says instead.

'How many small tings I can know? Lots-of happening in Goa today, Tony Calangute, lots-of. Policeman life not easy, no? So many peoples having accident, peoples fighting over property, all dis tourist peoples saying peoples cheating-cheating. Some tourist drowning also, swimming after drinking. Even off-duty I am on duty. Very busy.'

'Caetano, who is this handsome man?'

'Handsome, like tiatrist, no? Where dat cousin brudder? What his name is?'

'Dino.'

'Hoi, Dino. Always making problem for peoples.'

'What problem? Dino is no trouble to anybody.'

'Only to himself, aanh?' Fernandes laughs, taken with his joke.

The Amazon sulks. 'Caetano, are you going to introduce your friend?'

Tony can't immediately place the accent, and that bothers him. As innkeeper, he prides himself in locating nuances to the general vicinity, having already hosted flock from over sixty countries and the five continents. Then he homes in: with that pronunciation and bearing, it is most likely Brazilian.

'Sorry-no, dehling? Dis Tony Calangute.' PI Fernandes waves a hand in a flourish. 'And dis Princess.'

'My pleasure.' Tony shakes her hand with a lazy nod of his head. Her grip is capacious, firm, welcoming. 'Princess of...?'

'That is what I am called.'

'Ah, interesting.' Tony doesn't know what else to say. 'May I ask where you're from?'

'Brazil. In Goa everyone knows Brazil. Ronaldo, Ronaldinho,

Robinho, you people like football, crazy about football. I am from Bahia. You know Bahia? No? Only Rio, no? The world knows only Rio.'

'I'm sorry,' Tony is polite. 'But I hope you will tell me about Bahia—and Brazil. I have never been there. Welcome to Goa, Princess.'

'Muito obrigado. I have been here for some months already this year. This is my fourth season. Mostly I stay in the north. You speak Portuguese, my handsome hotel-man? Fala Português?'

'Um pouco.'

'He knows Portuguese,' Fernandes intervenes, irritated at being left out of the conversation. 'His type peoples all knows Portuguese. Like His Master's Voice. In old days dey speak Portuguese and be ruler. Like coconut, no? Brown outside, white inside. Viva Portugal! Viva *every*ting, men. Now *we* control, no? Common peoples, no big-big house peoples, no suit peoples. Now no Portuguese. Only Konknni and English and many Indu peoples speaking also Marathi. *What* you peoples do?' He puts a hand in front of Tony's face, fingers splayed like a fan. 'Nutting, no? Can do nutting!' Fernandes smiles.

Guests are turning to the table. Tony smiles at them and blocks PI Fernandes and the Princess as best as he can with his bulk.

'Where Dino?' Fernandes continues. 'I go to his house in Saligao but he not dere. His mummy said, Dino gone out. I tell to her, "You keep boy like good boy or he will damn bluddy get into troubles." She look so sad but what I do? I tell to her what I tell to her, no? You people still like brudders?'

He hooks his forefinger, commanding Tony to come closer. When he does, Fernandes drops his voice to a loud whisper. 'He making some big peoples angry. You tell him, go *slow*, men. More best, stop dis fool ting. You tell him go save birds and fish and all, not be like Jesus only. Only Jesus save peoples, not Dino Dantas. You know what 'appened Jesus? Work hard all lifes, doing magic and all and den put on cross wit big-big nails. Hairstyle be also gone to shits wit torns and all, no? What 'appened, only his mummy sad, no? Dino not save himself and he wants save peoples?'

'You tell him yourself,' Tony is smiling as he speaks. 'Why tell me all these things?'

'Because you listen, Tony Calangute, I hear dat from peoples. Dat Dino not listen. Dis not stupid ting like saving birds and all. Or closing small mines. Dis too big. *What* problem wit peoples coming here, having good time smoking-eating dis-dat? Buying land and all? Good for Goa, no? I'm not giving guarantee what happens when big peoples get angry. I am just policeman, not God and all. How much I do? Already I do too much only. What I get? New uniform. Can uniform be bangde fry? Can uniform be mackerel? Can uniform be Johnny-boy Black? You tell dat Dino. Nort Goa, Sout Goa, big peoples angry. One day someting happen and his mummy be sad for nutting…'

'Caetano is right. It is good for Dionysus to be careful,' the Princess adds in a murmur. 'These are troubled times. Family must take care of family.'

'Si. I will tell him. I don't know what you mean, but I will tell him.' Tony can barely breathe with anger and, inexplicably, fear that makes him want to rush to defecate. He knows now, for certain, that the reason for PI Fernandes's visit is only for the purpose of warning Tony about Dino; General Dantas must be getting too close to uncomfortable truths for a snake like Fernandes to show up knowing he would be unwelcome. But Tony forces himself to normality and unclenches his body. The snake and the snake lady seem to be partners. Still smiling, Tony straightens, unsure if Francesco would approve of what he is about to do. But PI Fernandes has crossed a line, and so shall he.

'We are busy tonight, so if y'all are done… Princess, thank you for coming.'

'My pleasure.' Tony can see she is surprised at the abrupt dismissal.

As he turns to go, PI Fernandes begins to tap the table with a forefinger. 'Ay, Tony Calangute? Dis bill?'

The music is being changed. There is a moment of perfect silence before conversation again steps into the breach. Tony chooses that moment to reply. 'You pay, Fernandes.' You can probably buy this place you thief-bastard, he screams silently.

He avoids PI Fernandes's murderous glare and the Princess's eyes—like the python's which they found in the back garden at home last monsoon, fat and slow with feeding on a string of piglets, or so it was presumed later as nobody could find the offspring of Melba's sow. Dino had arrived with a snake-catcher from the forest department and taken away the python to release into the forests of Mollem to the east before Melba could get one of her goats to kill the snake.

Heads turn as Tony strides out of Happy Bar, his smile now a grimace. For a change, you pay.

12. The Life and Times of Winston Almeida: III

The day he was invited to join the Greater Goa Chamber of Commerce, Industry and Industriousness, Winston ordered a pigling.

It was of pinkish, farmed stock, maintained for Goa's legion of overseas visitors—travellers as well as sons and daughters of the soil from around the globe—and celebrities and achievers from teeming New Delhi and Bombay and newly rampant Bangalore, globally aware folk who knew of American adages such as the true value of pork as 'the other white meat'. Winston heard of this reference in an American comedy show on cable and thought it quite clever. An event of this magnitude called for more than a faeces imbiber of a black swine from Aparanta's villages.

Lumena and Carla cured and stuffed the privileged child of a sow for an entire day. They lovingly applied marinade—a paste of boiled liver, kidney and garlic—to it. The sisters-in-law then filled the pigling with a mix of tomatoes, onions, breadcrumbs, potatoes, mandatory green chillies and a flourish of cinnamon. Lumena expertly sewed the opening in its stomach as Carla raised the legs of the animal and gently rested its small head with bewildered eyes in the crook of her arm.

Winston was very pleased with the outcome, especially the gourmet flourish of fresh, lemon-green apple from the People's Republic of China that Lumena had procured from the municipal market in Margao and delicately placed in the mouth of the upper-class swine. Indeed, so pleased, he wanted to put both Lumena and Carla—lesser in girth than Lumena but better endowed with 'boobies', as he had heard a British tourist describe such objects. But this being a day for generosity, he put away the thought of Carla, and put Lumena alone.

The Greater Goa Chamber of Commerce, Industry and Industriousness has an imposing façade, all too rare in a Panjim rapidly losing its rambling stone-and-plaster charm and tiled houses in kindergarten colours to helter-skelter constructions of concrete and glass. It resembled the façade of the lesser and competing chamber, which went without the appellations of 'Greater' and 'Industriousness', and was even more imposing. All burnished teak and leather-covered chairs, the hide cracked and softened with the moisture of time and the pressure of countless posteriors.

Winston, in white suit, shirt and two-toned shoes, was ceremoniously led up the gently curving wooden staircase to the meeting room, where the governing council would formally induct him. He was accompanied by Iosif, now adorned with a cream silk bandana on his head. Winston was shown to a seat opposite the head of the table and the president, the slender, gaunt Manoel Joao Carmelito Lourenco Estevam Jorge Rodrigo Cabral e Silva, from a family of fastidious traders. His name was emblazoned in full on a strip of gleaming brass on dark wood, ensuring in this burst of territoriality distance from his colleagues arrayed on either side. In contrast, his deputy and next in line for presidentship, the plump Nandu Zuarinagarcar, owner of vast mines of iron ore and shipping, occupied far less space on brass.

'Please,' said the president, or 'MJ', as he preferred to be called, graciously waving Winston to a chair. MJ's minutely curled lips betrayed a trace of annoyance at the culture of the chamber's newest inductee, exhibited in an attire more suited to a cadaver inside a coffin. Zuarinagarcar merely smiled. He had remained a man of few words in all his years of dedicated fornication with nature and being benevolent dictator to migrant labour from impoverished parts of India. Though separated by achievement and class, Winston nevertheless sensed in Zuarinagarcar a kindred spirit, a man who would rather use a gargantuan mechanized extractor where a petite shovel would do.

'Gentlemen,' said MJ, for in the Chamber's governing council there weren't any ladies, generally thought by the grandees as suitable only for putting and manufacturing babies. 'I would like to take this opportunity to welcome to our Chamber Senhor Winston Almeida, chairman, managing director and chief executive officer of Almeida Bros.'

Winston beamed at the polite applause, stopping only when Iosif's thunderclaps of appreciation went beyond manners.

'Quiet, no, id-*jut*,' he hissed, eyes close to clouding over with a premonitory red and blinking their terminal anger.

Iosif was immediately apologetic, and stood up to bow deeply in the general direction of MJ and Zuarinagarcar with a polite, 'Sorry, boss.'

MJ's lower lip, distended over the years with bouts of finger-pulling nervousness over the government's confusing import-export laws, elegantly trembled with disgust. He remained upright, determined suddenly to attack this thug and his intemperate sibling from the lower rungs of Goan society.

'Please Mr Almeida,' he invited. 'We all have heard so much about you. We would like to know your vision for the Chamber and, of course, for Goa. My colleagues and I are *very* interested.' And he thought: there, the lout will self-destruct in a minute. In that, MJ was wrong, and to all assembled it would soon become clear MJ was not in touch with realities of the day.

'Tank you tanks, MJ, sir,' Winston replied with a small bow, as gentlemen from Portuguese times would reserve for one another. He looked around the room before pronouncing the words that would in mere hours set afire Aparanta's media and corridors of power.

'I have dream, no?' he gravely ventured, and quickly realized those were not the words of his hero but of some American gentleman whose name he could not immediately recollect. That was an indicator it could not possibly have been a hero of the Great Wars, but some other deep conflict. But Winston recovered with aplomb. '*What* I bring to Chambers? Goa is needing bloods, tools, tears and sweats. We are having problems, lots-of lots-of problems. What we do? We make war on poor peoples only—not *on* poor peoples, but not *make* dem into poor peoples, no? We gives jobs, we makes peoples rich. And dis we do wit powers and strengths of God also. But He will only come for penalty kick, no?' Winston paused for breath, and observed a room in thrall.

'What our aim is? Victory only, Victory only for fit buggers. Survival of—dis ting—survival of fittest, I am telling y'all. Udderwise, Goa going nowhere. No ticket only, so how to go? Mummy, daddy, childrens, young peoples, all be sad, no? Dis my goal, not from penalty only, but straight, dribbling like centre forward, one-nil, two-nil, tree-nil! We must be Victorian! So y'all come and togedder like football team we go, all like centre forward, and score many goals for Goa. Great states. States for the peoples, lands for the peoples and powers for the peoples. Den only we all will be rich peoples and all. *Den* only,' Winston paused for impact. 'Viva Goa!'

The gathering listened with attention, for in the recent history of the Greater Goa Chamber of Commerce, Industry and Industriousness no one, least of all a new member, had made such an impassioned opening speech. When he rounded off his remarks with his trademark sign-off, pausing for a heartbeat before delivering the punchline, the chamber knew it had in its midst a future president.

'We needs POA for MOA,' Winston announced.

The room resounded with silence, while MJ's lips increased in tremble and Zuarinagarcar's smile increased in width. Iosif, as usual, came to the rescue. 'Plan of action,' he explained, and adjusted the bandana on his head, sneakily inserting a forefinger to savagely scratch a spot behind his right ear, a move that drew the attention of the entire room. He inspected his fingernail, flicked away the soggy clot of dead skin and explained the second part of the statement. 'Men of action, no?'

The chamber broke into loud applause, with the exception of MJ and Zuarinagarcar who responded with polite clapping and fixed smiles. The next day, the media set Winston's saying in stone. An article titled 'MOA with a POA' was placed as a boxed item on the front page of *Goa Chronicle,* alongside an analysis of the day's Number One in trouble, a brief update about a presumably drunk motorcyclist careening off the road past the small fish market under the Mandovi Bridge and into the poisoned river to his death; and an announcement of the arrival of Russian charter flights for the following season.

Winston did not miss the items about Number One and Russian charters despite obvious pleasure at reading about his conquest. The son of the demented Olimpio, and rampant MOA, had finally arrived in Goa Dourada.

13. A Little Something About Signs

Unlike my own home, Casa Esperança is a house bereft of tears, Tony thinks as he walks towards his office. At Casa Esperança, Gabru Dantas's dedication to a life and spouse he can barely fathom after decades of marriage, there is no time and place for such nonsense.

'They are like a women's cooperative,' Dino often tells Tony, with a few variations every now and then. 'Idiot men like us are lucky to have them. Just look at us—failed husbands, sons and fathers.' Tony would rarely offer anything in the face of this self-deprecatory storm and instead look to Francesco for a commandment: '*Why* bugger with the tides that God has given men, men? Better always to go with the flow, no?'

But Dino creates his own tides. He often wears a favourite T-shirt, blue with a two-line message in large white letters: SAVE GOA FROM GOANS. He also distributes these free to schoolchildren and college students of Aparanta and, for two hundred rupees, to anyone who will buy one at Save Goa Society's booth in the Anjuna flea market every Wednesday during the tourist season, or directly from the Society's modest office in Panjim. There are more, in different colours and with different messages. SAVE GOA FOR OUR CHILDREN. SAVE GOA FROM MINEFIELDS. SAVE GOA, SPEAK UP! There are cartons of these piled up at the office and even in the storeroom at the back of Casa Esperança in Saligao, displacing many racks of Gabriel's legal reference at Ida's pleasure. And so Dino preaches his fire, and begs children and adults alike to convert to the religion of Aparanta. To save their land. To preserve their dignity.

'Are you a signboard?' a disgusted Gabriel asked him from time to time. But Anjali loved the shirts as they were comfortable to sleep in, and had demanded her own set. She had also taken to wearing them outside the house, which truly upset Gabriel because neighbours and others would ask about his granddaughter wearing messages, unbecoming for children from the finer houses of Aparanta. When he took these tales to Ida and Dino, Ida would rage as Dino looked on with an amused expression, hearing his mother rail about how the men of Goa did not have balls. She used Portuguese gutterspeak for this—'Não têm colhões!' At this Gabriel would flinch, because Ida did not usually question by implication the manhood of Aparanta, only its intellect and purpose. But when he challenged her, she would expand her diatribe, talk of the times when good Goans—Hindu, Catholic or Muslim—would take to the sword, writing or vocal protest, any form of resistance, if they did not like what Portuguese or any dominion had brought on them. That the table of the Inquisition, which now few bother to visit in its ignored resting place in Panjim, accounted for the blood of more Goans than any war, that the jails of Aparanta, Angola and Portugal had been packed with patriots who wanted Aparanta to live on her own terms. If her son and her granddaughter wanted to wear shirts with a message to convey that Aparanta wanted her share from robbers of her grave, they would do so. If Advogádo Dantas and his army of the seeing-blind did not like it they could go and drown themselves in the Mandovi. That would be an easy enough task, Ida thundered, what with the garbage, faeces and bilge, from Panjim, a hundred villages and endless barges, that daily find their way to the river, enough to send clams into toxic shock.

'Dissent can be good,' Ida insisted. 'We need to exercise some of the fish curry and rice that is supposed to make us so clever, no?

May God bless Goa.'

Gabru, with nothing more to say, would turn to Francesco for support. And after Francesco went, he would retreat to his practice or his study. Gabru did that a lot these days, Tony knew, as Dino would tell him, 'Dad acts like he can't handle us any more. He hasn't been the same since I came back from Bombay and after Christabel left.'

Gabru Dantas, the cousins agreed, had simply given up trying to understand the disturbed orbits of his once orderly life.

14. Dionysus Tells Some Folk Tales

In Tony's office, Dino is on the computer, his weapon of choice, what he calls the 'web of the world to trap spiders', to reach out to allies across Perpet Saibinn's earth. Tony suspects more missives have been planned and executed here these past two years than at Save Goa Society's tiny office in Panjim, or at Casa Esperança.

Dino looks up calmly, doesn't waste time with pleasantries. 'Our friend said something to you.'

'You know Fernandes is here?' Tony is incredulous.

'Hmm.' Dino plucks at the small knot of hair under his lip that resembles fishing lure. 'Saw him at the bar on my way in. He must have been waiting for me. That's why I came to your office.'

'What the hell have you been doing?' Tony cannot contain himself any more. This is no time to curry favour with the Saibinn. He will later, and light some candles at her altar. Perhaps he should ask Umesh to get him a few dozen. The way things are going, the petite Saibinn will be covered in wax from head to toe and be protected from damp and pollution from the smoke-belching buses that son-of-a-mongoose Nini Braganza owns. Next time he sees Nini, Tony has a good mind to rip out a pressure horn and put it up his bum so when he walks people will know from the noise Nini is nearby and leave a wide arc so as not to step on his shadow. And for that act of kindness old Tefu Pereira will look upon him as a son.

'Control yourself, dear boy,' Dino smirks. 'If you explode, you will splatter across everything and spoil this charming room.' Dino is too calm.

'What is happening, Dino? Why is he here? Who is that woman with him?'

'You really don't know what's going on, do you?'

'I run a small hotel, you fool.' Tony walks to his desk and sits across from Dino. He rubs his fingers across his forehead so hard it feels like the skin will peel from his skull. 'I hear what I need to hear.'

Tony knows there is as little chance of escaping Dino as there is of his escaping his life. For a few years Dino was away, because Ida insisted her son would not be trapped in Goa 'and get an island mind'. But he came back from Bombay, still tied to Ida and Goa, a sullen wife with him, leaving behind the possible life of riches and fame his engineering college had a reputation for securing its graduates—an American or Australian passport, or at least Portuguese, because those tripas-eaters are part of the European Union and that makes it easy to travel and work there. The gossip drums of Aparanta had for a while written off Dino's return as nothing more than a silly boy's declaration of war, his anger to be dissipated by time and ennui. 'And look at what he called his organization—Save Goa Society.' A distant aunt, Ana-Maria, had even snorted at Ida as the family gathered for Ana-Maria's seventy-fifth birthday: 'Your son, no? What he tink he is? Mr Jesus Christ? *Saving* Goa and all? Silly, no?'

It had been within earshot of Tony, and he had seen the icy anger on Ida's face, knowing she would maintain peace on account of the occasion as much out of politeness, because Ana-Maria was related to Gabru. Tony had wondered about what Ana-Maria had said of Dino, as he had once thought the very same thing. But when he had brought it up with Dino, his cousin dismissed it saying people sometimes needed a dramatic name, as much as dramatic purpose to propel it. That had been nearly eight years earlier; at that time Tony hadn't given Dino more than a year to realize his folly and head back to Bombay to resume a life interrupted by emotion.

But Dino is here, and so is he. Tony sits numbly to listen to the folk tales of Dionysus of Aparanta.

◆

The Dino-rant is a thing of wonder. Delicate fingers are placed on both temples, like a person cannibalizing his own spirit. The head is lowered, eyes are half-closed and words delivered in a monotone for the first few minutes as Dino-rant gathers force. Tony knows he will then pound his forehead with the heels of his palms, pull furiously at his beard, in particular the fish lure, pace the room in a frenzy until he is drained for the time of all that flails at him, demons in his every atom.

'What the Yakuza, Japanese gangsters with a predilection for tattoos, did to Hawaii is what the sons of Lenin and Stalin want to do here,' Dino tells him.

'They want it all. They want to build hotels, resorts and clubs, bring in pleasure women and men, trance, everything. They even control the charter businesses, which brings along with a fig leaf a captive audience. They want to plough the cunt of Goa while she lies back like a whore fuelled by ecstasy. Lies back and enjoys it even,' Dino brutally insists, 'all the while deluding herself that she's doing the world a favour by hosting it while in reality she is already carrion, ripe and peeling.

'Visitors come to Aparanta for instant therapy, but what of our illness, what of our poison that mixes with the poison of visitor residue? We are steeped in toxicity and yet so few notice.' He exhales, 'The couch itself is in need of therapy.' Tony attempts an explanation, but Dino waves him to silence, knowing what it will be: that innkeepers of Aparanta can do little if the rulers of Aparanta do little.

Tony watches Dino slowly unfold from the chair and stand, turn left to walk towards the door, check his face in a small decorative mirror on the wall and abruptly turn around like a wound-up toy soldier.

'It all happens on Goenchi mati and sons and daughters of the soil support it,' Dino feeds on his anger. 'Sons and daughters of the soil are the creators and beneficiaries of this garbage. The panchas who act big when a crow takes a shit on a coconut without asking, disappear when it is time to decide if they care about their village, or the next elections…anyway, all that is no longer the decision of the panchayat, but of the Number Ones and Winstons.'

So the good sons and daughters of the soil elected to protect their villages wilfully look away as their beaches of gold are stolen every night by bullock carts. The trucks that once aided in the rape and transport of sand have now been cleverly banished in favour of the noiseless and easily camouflaged carts, Tony hears from Dino. Villagers don't dare to complain against the sand thieves, fearful of real estate sharks that back them, and the shores of Aparanta crumble in despair. The sons and daughters of the soil also share the spoils of one rave in dream-weaver drugs—more than what the Villa will make in an entire season. With ready conspirators, why will the new conquistador, not walk with heads held high, their jewels and mansions, mistresses and SUVs, symbols of acquisition as potent as the riches that once fed Portugal's empire?

'With that amount of money, who is going to shut them up? The line goes straight to the top.' Dino is close to hysteria. The panchayat can't stop it, or won't stop it, the police won't do anything. *Why* should anyone stop it? We go around blaming the world, the bhaille'—Dino uses the derogatory word for 'outsiders'—'but the snakes are here in Eden, brother mine.'

PI Fernandes is a manager more than a policeman, Dino insists, manager for people like Winston, who are no longer happy confined to Salcette and are running short of land to pillage. There are now too many little Winstons—he has inspired an entire tribe. He needs to expand into new areas and those like Fernandes help him. Dino is jabbing the air with his right forefinger like a prosecuting lawyer, but he has only his demons and Tony for company. 'Winston wants some action in north Goa. I heard that he got Fernandes transferred to Narcotics and that hyena is going around to almost all the coastal villages across Chapora River under some pretext or the other to negotiate for land on behalf of a consortium Winston is part of.'

'What for?' Tony mumbles, weak with ache.

'What for?' Dino is too agitated to sit down. 'Bloody Winston is going to do business with the Russians for drugs and land. One feeds the other. The Israelis are relatively small fish, everybody knows that. If they, the Nigerians or anyone else get in the way, the Russians will flay their skin and make decorative yin-yang bags to sell at the Saturday-night market.' Those who really control the trade are low-key, he says. They are deep inside the quieter vaddos of Anjuna, Chapora, Vagator, places further north. 'Fernandes must be losing his mind with all that money he makes,' Dino suggests, 'or he would never be seen together with that Amazon. She—or he—is a front for the Russians.'

'The Princess?' Tony is relieved to find something he can deal with. 'These days it's difficult to make out who is *what*, men. You should see some of the people who come to the Villa.' He absently reaches across to take a paper napkin from the lacquer box on the side of his desk and slowly wipes the top.

Dino is smiling. 'The earnest innkeeper.'

'What else would I do? Become like you?'

'How are things at home?'

'Go to hell.' Tony looks at his hands.

'Anastasia is at our place a lot these days. Anjali and her Nasty-mummy seem to be getting along very well. It's good, no? Anjali needs a mother, and I'm hardly much of a father.'

'All that unused mother's love has to mean something, no? It's a blessing,' Tony says in a small voice, his head bowed low. 'And you? What about Tilly and you? She's not like some of the others you have met at Happy Bar.'

'What the...?' Dino instinctively begins in angry counterattack, then calms down, sensing his cousin's meaning. 'It's called "need", Tony. We seem to need each other. We're figuring each other out, not loved-up yet or anything. Since you asked, I haven't felt this way about anyone since Charming. The attraction is instinctive, almost animal.'

Tony is silent. Dino rarely talks about Charming de Souza in this vein these days—a former girlfriend and now ally from Varca, Winston's den, who regularly contributes money to the Save Goa Society from her furniture business.

'What does Tilly say?' he finally asks.

'What is there to say? We're two drifters who have come together. We're only flotsam, my friend.'

'Seems to work for some people,' Tony chokes, 'All this love thing.'

'Look at us,' General Dantas allows after a moment of silence. 'Brothers-in-arms.'

15. Great Games

When Tony finally looks up, unmindful of time having passed, he notices Dino's slumped form. Oh, Saibinn, he marvels. Must be the strain of carrying the weight of the world, he thinks in a moment of viciousness, before he pushes the thought away.

'Fernandes said you're upsetting big people,' Tony offers.

Dino says he does not have enough fingers to list the reasons. He suggests the Princess is with the Russians because she can't fight them, and few can—they are powerful, numerous and vicious, leading a pack of wolves that now freely roam the world. People like the Princess are better off being intermediaries for deals, Dino says, in turn she lives an unfettered life in Aparanta by the Sea. Winston is their front for buying land because they need an ambitious son of the soil to own it for them, if need be, and certainly clear the way for toehold and growth. But first, there is need to convert forest and farmland for commercial use. Number One is agreeable to this. Maybe he needs the money to buy fellow lawmakers—vermin for hire. Or maybe he is just tired of his collection of Mont Blanc pens and wants a new collection of something more exotic. If new real estate developments of the nature that is being heard of in Morjim and Mandrem go through, even a small percentage of the cut will be worth tens of millions over time to Number One.

'I am in the way, and a few others like me,' Dino then says. 'We weren't many to begin with, and there are fewer of us each day, at the Society and elsewhere. I wonder if fear saps them, or they are bought out, or just tired. I know I am, man. So fucking tired.'

He looks out of the small window at the strolling crowds on the road, back from dinner at teeming shacks along the beach. The crowds in Sodomo are indicative of the growing mix, Indian and overseas travellers in a more relaxed mood now that the sun has set, and with it the curious need to control the beaches that visitors displayed with increasing belligerence in the war of the World versus Aparanta.

His days are now spent talking to the panchayats in Morjim and Mandrem and even places further north like Keri, Dino tells Tony. His colleagues at Save Goa Society get small groups of villagers together to try and convince them not to sell out to Winston and his cohorts and radiate that feeling outwards, convince more people, pressure the panchayats to see the wisdom of this way or risk losing their land and livelihood to the empire of concrete and trance. But it's a losing battle, Dino sighs. There is no power on earth that can prevent enrichment, or take away the lure of money from those who have either too little or too much. There is no option but to take it to the law of the land, petition courts to intercede on behalf of Aparanta. This Dino has done, and will continue to do as long as he is able.

'I'm not surprised some people are upset,' Dino sighs. 'They are even trying to sway some of my colleagues, mainly the board of trustees. And they will sway, the congenital fucks. They have too much to lose.'

Dino looks to Tony for approval, but Tony is too tense to do anything except remain motionless, like a man who fears movement will upset the fragile balance of his world. There are many worlds in Aparanta, and all are being breached—who will presume to prevent Winston when there are as many barbarians inside the gates of Aparanta as outside?

Dino is saying he had written an article for *Goa Chronicle* the previous weekend, a continuation in outrage to the first, published a weekend earlier, about increasing lawlessness in Goa. Tony has read both. The second was about how some established business families, including that of an early Number One, had run riot in east and southeast Aparanta, absorbing vast tracts of jungle, some with the claim that they had family temples in those places, removed to remote locations in the days of persecution by the Portuguese. All this with complicity of the state. Dino's article called it grand thievery, to tear more ore for hungry factories in the Orient, to tear stone for hungry Winstons to build and build and build. Soon there would be little left of Aparanta below the ground and above it. And this was happening as citizens of Aparanta saw yet they did not, heard yet they remained deaf, and, as for speaking, why waste precious breath?

The articles had slipped through because Dino had undertaken the ruse of delivering them at the very last minute, knowing well they would otherwise raise chaos at *Goa Chronicle* even before the paper ran them, and calls would be placed to several generous, soon-to-be livid concessionaires of Aparanta.

Armando Rodrigues, the editor of *Goa Chronicle,* had gently accosted Dino on the steps of Clube Vasco da Gama in Panjim the previous week. Dino was on his way in for a beer—just a beer, he had promised himself—before going to Casa Esperança for a few rare moments with Anjali. Editor Rodrigues was heading home to dinner after a few large measures of 'Russian feni', as he gleefully termed it, accompanied by a snack of roasted ox tongue, leaving his minions to put to bed his fattened newspaper. Fattened further only a few hours previously, as Dino had discovered from a friend at the paper.

Number One's personal assistant had conveyed a message to Editor Rodrigues within the friend's earshot earlier that day. 'Why you do like this, Mr Rodricks, writing bad tings about boss and friends? Your press working full-time? You not wanting printing order, advertising also?' The man had even injected humour with promised funds. 'How it hurts, some words making holiday? Goa is holiday destination, no? Number one, no?' (A practical man, Editor Rodrigues had agreed. Within a week the pages of *Goa Chronicle* would be filled with advertisements, as if the monsoon had ended and the fishing boats returned again to the jetties, low in the water with fruits of the sea. The government printing order, he was told, would land any day.)

On the dingy, betel juice-stained staircase, Editor Rodrigues had called Dino aside to say he had been getting calls not to publish Dino's articles in 'public interest', because Goans needed to hear 'Good things only, no? And bugger all this devil-bad news. Why not paint the future and all with a rainbow and give people hope?' That is why he would be unable to any longer publish what Dino wrote, unless Dino corrected his ways, let fire and brimstone be, took a vacation from words.

When Dino pressed his point, Editor Rodrigues mumbled a homily about how the greater good of Goa comes before the individual wishes of a few. Dino then mentioned mildly *that* was exactly what he wanted to say, only Editor Rodrigues and he appeared to be on either side of a chasm with their definitions of 'few', but the man had continued his meandering journey down the steps, ricocheting off a wall to slingshot his way around a corner. Dino had followed him, angry now, accusing the editor of a compact with the likes of Number One. The compact with Winston he already knew about, Dino said.

'Dino Dantas, you're a brave idiot. Why don't you let Gabru Dantas and that mother of yours sleep in peace? How does it hurt to be quiet for a few months, no?' Editor Rodrigues continued in parting.

Be quiet for a few months. Why bother with Number Ones, present and past? Why, indeed, bother with Winston? Wasn't he a true son of the soil? Didn't he bring a future for Aparanta?

With this, Dino is done, and slides down the side of a wall to sit on his haunches, staring at Tony like a man who needs to spend a few days in his beloved hills to the east, perhaps near the forgiving source of the Mandovi. Take the roads that embrace the green, soaring over the estuaries of Aparanta's muddy-red rivers, past the faded glories of Old Goa.

Dino's tales suggest to Tony a world he has always kept at arm's length. It is more complex than bribing thieves from the electricity department and telephone companies to repair disconnects at the Villa. Or keeping away MB's aggressive entreaties for Tony to send guests to Boom Shack and share the wealth from travellers 'like a good Indian'. It is nothing like fighting the pestilence of the sow-cockroach Melba, and more perplexing than living with the shards of his marriage to Anastasia and their grieving, desperate hearts. Dino's tales are beyond the comforting shadows of Francesco's commandments and the Saibinn's unwavering generosity.

'What will you do?'

'I can't stop, Tony. If I stop now—we stop now—it's over,' Dino raises his head. 'I have to try and smoke the bastards out.'

'You're alone.'

'I'm not alone, Tony. I could never have held out for this long had I been alone. Others are doing good work, but we are too few. There are fieldworkers at the Society who have far less than what I have but they are the brave ones, I could not have made any headway in the villages if my staff and volunteers weren't there to help, poor people, kids—students. I sometimes worry more about my fattened trustees than I do about anything else. The privileged are always more slippery.'

'What will you do?' Tony asks again.

'I don't know,' Dino smiles his Ida-smile, it is for the viewer to discern disdain or warmth, and Tony chooses warmth. 'It doesn't matter.'

16. The Life and Times of Winston Almeida: IV

Over the years, Winston Almeida had grown used to instant compliance and adulation. Like a true achiever, he did not care if such action and emotion came from genuine belief or genuine fear. And, like a true leader, he quickly became a legend in his own mind. This was in keeping with a key premise embedded in principles of management: that staunch, even violent self-belief is a prerequisite for leadership. But Winston had no real need of such amateurism. He had as guide his namesake, whose teachings, combined with Winston's own feral instincts, were enough.

After his celebrated conquest of the Greater Goa Chamber of Commerce, Industry and Industriousness, Winston rapidly gained in stature. People came to him for advice. His name began to appear in textbooks as a true son of Goan soil. He received invitations from all eleven talukas of Goa, in his own words, from the revenue district of Pernem in 'Indu-bugger nort' to Canacona in 'Indu-bugger sout' to Quepem in 'Indu-bugger sout of east, no?' and, of course, from the snugly 'Catlick' heartland of the Velhas Conquestas of Ilhas, Bardez, Mormugao and his home taluka of Salcette, where special attention was reserved for him.

A cartoon in *Goa Chronicle* that dared deride him as a son of the night soil led to prompt repercussion: the cartoonist lost his job the following day. This was on account of a threat to withdraw a year's worth of advertising that heralded a new complex of luxury houses by Almeida Bros, its foundation laid after gouging out an entire forested hillside near Dona Paula. It once belonged to the people of Odxel, who were coerced to sell at suppressed prices. '*What* bluddy damn and all dat-dat-dat?' Winston had roared at Editor Rodrigues over the telephone, reminding him of their arrangement, and how Editor Rodrigues had made quite a killing by offloading at great profit an apartment Winston had sold him at far below market rate. 'You fucking me, I fucking you.'

This crystal clear message prompted an end to all manner of cartoons in *Goa Chronicle,* which indirectly earned Winston much goodwill from other thugs—those barely off the streets as well as those ensconced formerly and currently as Number One.

Winston presided at the annual day of schools, cut ribbons to inaugurate modest buildings to house various village panchayats, saving the grandest one, in Varca, to be built with his own hard-earned money, of which a large component comprised other people's hard-earned money. But leaders would not be leaders if they permitted trivia to cloud their vision, and Winston had the eyes of a hawk. He inaugurated hardware stores, men's tailoring shops and modest beauty salons, permitting Lumena for the first—and, as it happened, the last—time in his life to share the limelight with him, as it was now appropriate to publicly smoothen his rough edges.

Lumena's misery in her brutal life with Winston was partially offset when she saw her photograph in *Goa Chronicle* for the first time, smiling more graciously than her by-now imperious husband. The caption elaborated: 'Builder, firebrand leader and true son of the soil Winston Almeida cutting ribbon to inaugurate Reissa's Beauty Palace for Mens and Womens in Margao, also having branch near Maria Hall, Benaulim. A smiling Mrs Lumena and the famous Miss Reissa da Costa, Muscat-returned (right), owner of Beauty Palace, are also seen.'

Winston had come upon Lumena smiling over it the following day, showing the photograph to their three boys who in turn were delighting in this minor joy in their mother's gritty life. Incensed that she had dared to read the newspaper before he had—a rule Lumena had inadvertently forgotten in her happiness at her first stab at public glory—Winston had lashed out with the back of his hand, snagging his gold ring in the large ruby in Lumena's right nostril and tearing it as he disengaged. Somehow Lumena managed to save the photograph from the torrent of blood that poured from her, and ten-year-old Tojo quickly took it from his mother's hand and ran to the toilet to get a towel to soak her spill. Tito, a year younger, hugged his hysterical mother to prevent further onslaught by his father, bloodying his prized T-shirt bought on a rare trip with his cousins—Iosif's son, Lenin, and daughter, Nikita—to nearby Colva beach, with a simple message, 'Goa…Come to Paradise' below a smiling sun, two gracefully arched coconut palms and three wavy lines of deep blue sea. Young Tarzan, all of eight—the serial age of the brothers indicative of Winston's persistent putting before Lumena's clever severing of her tubes—had rushed at his father and butted him in the privates with his head. Winston had collapsed, clutching his putting equipment, screaming 'Fodrechea!' over and over again as he rolled this way and that on the floor of the living room, with its mosaic of the Al U emblem. Old enough to know he was being called a cunt by another name, Tarzan had again run at his father, and this time kicked him in the same spot, a tactic he sometimes employed with goalkeepers in the parish playground whenever they fell at his feet to clutch a dangerous football.

Winston had passed out from the pain and shock at being hit by the boy he had named after a half-naked savage he had read about in the books, who swung from trees dressed in leopard skin but was really a lost Lord of the Realm from the same land as Winston's hero. Lord Greystoke must have been made up, Winston thought before losing consciousness while cradling his crotch: Would a real lord kick his own father in the balls?

From that day, for all purposes, Winston forgot he had a wife and children. He never again directly exchanged a word with them, including at table and even during family occasions. He began to spend more time away from home, eventually taking up residence whenever he wished at one of the luxury cottages he had built on a stretch of land overlooking the lovely island of St Jacinto in the estuary of the Zuari River. It was land he had a bureaucrat in Panjim, Mandar Gaonkar, convert from protected forest to 'suitable for construction', the official made pliant with the discovery by a resourceful Iosif of misdemeanours on a previous posting, such as misappropriation of funds meant to develop village schools. Of course, the move to convert Mandar Gaonkar had been greatly boosted by Vimochan Sardessai, influential minister of town and country planning and forests, in the Cabinet of Number One. In turn, Vimochan Sardessai accepted from Winston a cottage in the name of his wife Urmila. To sweeten the deal, there was an extended weekend of discreet putting—along with Winston—in a small but comfortable and tucked-away hotel on the Juhu seafront in Bombay, and later in Dubai, away from the prying and ungrateful eyes of the electorate. Their compact was to them a sign of a deep sense of harmony among the Hindus and Catholics of Goa.

'All dese id-*juts,*' Winston had explained in righteous anger after they had completed a glorious late seafood and tandoori dinner at their penthouse suite at Good View Hotel. Alongside, there was a bottle of Johnny Gold, a perfect way to cap an evening of ménage à quatre with two slender Nepali girls overjoyed with a thousand-rupee tip—five hundred each. 'What dey tink? Catlick peoples and Indu peoples not together? Dey not going to fest of St Anne in Talaulim looking for husbands and wifes and childrens? Dey not going to Indu house in Panjim with Good Friday pro-say-shun? Indu peoples not giving cunji for Siridao chapel fest? Indu peoples and Catlick peoples not dancing like mad peoples for Siolim zagor?'

'Dancing, of course, dancing,' Vimochan Sardessai had agreed, his mind reeling with the double joys of Johnny Gold and coitus, idly fondling the buttocks of one girl, his fingers now circling the ring of her anus, now her vagina, as she and her associate gorged on chicken tandoori.

Warming to the theme of coexistence, Winston had taken the next step in his meteoric career. 'Dis not like brudders, putting together?' he had asked.

'Hoi, like brothers only,' the minister had cautiously agreed.

Sensing an opening, Winston made his move. 'We like team, like football team. You honourable minister, I honourable businessman. We make team, no? Like my Al U. Only dis Goa U. I grows, you grows, we all grows.'

'Hoi,' Vimochan Sardessai had agreed, and suddenly stopped fondling the girl when he realized through his daze that Winston, whom he privately thought of as little more than an insect, a person he could do business with and even share prostitutes with in the same room, but never invite to his unsullied Saraswat Brahmin home, was driving a bargain. 'What you want?' he asked, on guard.

'Nutting brudder,' Winston said, all humility. 'I want to share, no? In business it is good to grow big? But *how* I grows? All dese peoples, Dempo, Salgaoncar, Chowgule, Timblo, Menezes, dis-dat, dey have everyting, no, from mining to shining? Some from Portuguese times also. *What* I have? Few buildings only. I grows in new ways, no?' Winston marked the reasons by thrusting out three fat fingers in turn from a closed fist. 'New land. New business. New money. I am making some new friends, some Russian peoples. Lots of money, no? Dey have dere friends. Some police peoples are wit me also. You talk to boss, no? I keeps you happy, I keeps him happy—*what* matters?'

'What we do in Dubai? Ticket confirmed, no? First-class?' Vimochan Sardessai had finessed, pleased that Winston recognized his proximity to Number One and equally eager, in the role of power broker, to exploit Winston's greed.

'We do what you wants, brudder. Your first time in Dubai, no? I go many times. We go to Jumeirah, and stay dis nice big-big hotels, buy gold tings for your Mrs. Gold good for keeping mouth shut. Den someting for you, dat fat-fat pen wit white flower on top of cap all dese big peoples are carrying, dis blank-blank ting. Me also, or dey tink I be small peoples—*mad* bluddy peoples, dis, but what to do?' Winston took a deep sip of Johnny Gold after pouring more soda into the glass. 'We have first-class fun. We open bank account also, no? Why to have problems in Goa? We grows and your ten per cent also grows. Dats why I go to Dubai. Good banks. Good also for kebabs,' Winston grinned hugely, and neatly plucked one of the girls, put her mouth over his slyly rampant penis and forced her down. Not quite done with her meal, she squealed in surprise and pain. 'See, dis like T.C.,' Winston gloated with lust. Realizing Iosif was not at hand to explain acronyms, he proclaimed: 'Tandoori chicken, no?'

Vimochan Sardessai was stunned. But not to be outdone by this lout who, he had to nevertheless admit, possessed cunning as well as an interesting profile in debauchery, Vimochan Sardessai grabbed his girl by the hips and vigorously rubbed himself against her to gain an erection—as impressive as Winston's, he thought—and entered her as quickly as his overworked penis would permit. He then did what Winston would remember and subsequently attempt with varying degrees of success with prostitutes and mistresses: Vimochan Sardessai commanded the girl to rotate on his penis, like a merry-go-round.

'Good techniques, brudder,' Winston had to admit.

And so a grand alliance of political economy was formed, one that would soon encompass Number One. As professional thugs knew, as did professional managers, the wisdom of lateral thought to fuel Winston's grandest dream of conquering north Goa was being set in motion. With Number One behind him, Vimochan Sardessai strategically behind each tree plump with pickings, PI Fernandes and his Brazilian friend plugged into every purchase in soft sand and hard earth, and the eager, delirious Russians finally able in the Great Game to reach the shores of the Arabian Sea.

Meanwhile, as the wheels of such momentous events were set in motion, Lumena and her sons were immeasurably relieved that Winston visited them less and had even less to do with them. Winston ensured a façade was preserved by discreetly providing maintenance to his wife and sons, delivered through the sympathetic Iosif. The family appeared together for the briefest possible moments at parish events—or openings of businesses that had grown more numerous with an enhanced economy.

For Winston, it was a curious arrangement considering his ungrateful family and sons he would have killed with his bare hands had they been anybody else's but his own. But he knew the church and the state would intervene, unlike with the imperious lions of Africa that go about snapping the necks of cubs, sometimes their own, if they dare to stand in the way or bite their bum too hard at frolic. Winston wondered if his hero and namesake had felt this way after the great war, when the British public had forsaken their brilliant wartime prime minister to elect a man with no taste for power and brutal vision, just tame peace.

17. Visions in Sodomo

Tony Calangute has come to the sea, as he does in times such as these, when he needs to unburden one thing or another: Melba, Anastasia's onions and, now, Dino's crusades and his own sense of helplessness.

He is accompanied by Zezito, who carries a picnic basket of the Villa's best cashew feni, an icebox, a plain glass, a bottle of water, a few slices of bright yellow lemon bursting with lusciousness and acid, a folding chair and a small folding table. For the sake of form, Zezito has also brought along a small red-and-white checked tablecloth, faded with use, comforting in the way such things can be.

Happy Bar had quietened suddenly, as it always did, changing swiftly from a sanctuary of activity to accepting the death of the night. Residents at the Villa and visitors emptied the bar in noisy flight, triggered typically by one large group that departed to signal an end to festivities and forgetting for the day. It was like a tap being turned off by a mysterious force, and it never failed to amaze Tony. PI Fernandes and the Princess had fortunately disappeared without causing the Professor or Zezito grief over the bill. And Dino was last seen in animated and close conversation with Tilly, his new muse.

'I just want to live a little,' Tony had overheard Tilly saying to Dino. Dressed in a peacock-blue sarong, she had flapped her hands in the short, choppy strokes of a fledgling. 'I want to see if this girl can fly.'

She had smiled. 'I need to work on my technique. What do you think, Dino?'

'Why did you come here?' General Dantas wanted to know.

'Why does anyone come here, dammit?' Tilly had retorted, as if a little disappointed by the question. 'I can be myself without the great Indian moral indignation taking a shit on my head. If I smoke or talk to strangers I am not instantly labelled a bitch or a whore. As yet, I haven't been raped here or set on fire for dressing the way I do.'

'Brochure Goa,' Dino had grinned, and Tony thought they deserved each other. 'If you move two kilometres inland, it's a different world. Goa can choke you even as it frees you.'

Tony had lost the rest as he walked on. Dino had presumably taken himself back to Villa Esperança, to be sternly welcomed by Ida, who would not sleep until her tormented son returned home each night—even when he came home with the sun behind his back, parting the heavy morning air with his ancient Fiat.

Dino would spend entire days chasing the ghosts of Aparanta, spending hours with the police as they interviewed and counselled a gypsy child, a Lamani, or the offspring of a once-proud Rajasthani farmer shattered with poverty, raped by her Goan or bhaille neighbour; the roots of the violator—local or outsider—hardly mattered any more except for the sake of the age-old argument of who was doing it to whom. At other times, he would be livid after a meeting of the board of Save Goa Society, society matrons and self-proclaimed intellectuals concerned with praising one another's articles in *Goa Chronicle* and filling the pages with angst about how a paradise was slowly being lost, reiterating that outsiders were responsible but suggesting little by way of solution. It was an assertion so blind in denial that the only way to absorb it, according to Dino, was to storm off to Happy Bar, any bar, and let off steam. But he would never drive home in a state, nor would he accept hospitality at the Villa. So Dino Dantas, self-appointed scourge of the fat cats of Aparanta, would pass the night in the back seat of his ancient Fiat, curled in foetal sleep until crows, roosters and sugar-voiced bulbuls woke him.

In the mornings Villa Esperança dressed for a wedding, with frail jewels of white, orange and fuchsia bougainvillea, and the occasional scarlet or peach hibiscus, scattered across the front of the house. They would lie untouched for Anjali or Ida to collect before Geeta the maid swept them away. Anjali particularly liked bougainvillea to pour from her hands, repeating the motion in an unending stream of colour, and Dino would sometimes see her that way when he returned after a night of unrepentant unburdening, her enquiring eyes filled with concern and hurt.

'The day it changes to pity, I've lost her, brother mine,' Dino would tell Tony. 'Anjali means "offering to the gods" in Sanskrit. Tony, did you know that?'

And this romantic fool, the Saibinn bless him, was now bringing visitations from hell into Tony's world. The procession of two makes its way past the winding road north towards Sodomo creek, replete with now closed handicrafts and provision stores, past closed shacks that, to Tony's disgust, serve French fries with everything, from grilled kingfish to tempered xacuti.

Tony and Zezito reach the headland, where fishing boats are beached. Only a few stray dogs are awake to watch them. One barks lazily, and when Zezito silences it, saying he will trace its last five generations to castrate every male in the family that has not yet been run over by Nini Braganza's buses, the dun-coloured dog whines into silence, lowering its head to rest between its paws, eyes wrenchingly sad. Zezito folds out the table and chair a little distance away from the pack, closer to the rocks near the mouth of the creek, near a few orange and white fibreglass fishing boats. With a ceremonial flourish he places the tablecloth, pats down the corners, and waits for Tony.

'Zezito,' Tony says on cue. 'Go home now.'

'Patrao, if you do like this…'

'It's not like I do this everyday, old friend. Feni is a healer of wounds.'

'And it opens others.'

'You should take over from the Professor, and save us all. Go home, Zezito. I'll be fine. It's too late for tourists and too early for thieves.'

Zezito withdraws with a shake of the head to disappear between the shacks, taking care to sidestep the collection of plastic bottles, glass shards from flung bottles of beer and other alcohol, wrappers of confectionery and American-style wafers, the odd streamer of toilet paper and other remains of the day.

It is dark, the moon too weak in its crescent to let anything but the faintest silver tinge the surf. Palm trees hush their song. Gradually, everything recedes from Tony. The hill to his right with a retreat for Jesuit fathers shrouded in green on all sides and open to the ocean in front. The creek, now fattened with incoming tide. The blue-on-white sign of Milly & Johnny's Ye Olde Sandwich Shoppe across the creek. The white boat named after the Lady of Vailankanni and the orange one by its side painted with lesser blessings—Dominic and Fly—but bursting with pride of achievement.

To the left, the trance-madness in Mambo Lane at the borderlands of Sodomo and Calangute would have ended. Disc jockeys on a sabbatical from Ibiza and Berlin, young achievers from India's great cities and visitors from the world would be preparing to retire in the afterglow of desperate tribal celebration and mating rituals, still restless with whimsical energy, as if the following day air would be sucked out of their bodies, and their hearts switched off without warning. (Tony had once read about bullfrogs in the Kalahari Desert that come out during the few hours of rain after years of hibernation in drought. They must—before the water vanishes and their lives again withdraw to nothingness—refresh, mate and eat.) A frenzy of trance rituals, as if the earth wasn't burdened enough with pheromone. And the smell, by the Saibinn's blessed nose; if they wanted their mating so much they could at least make use of the sea to cleanse!

It is a void, and Tony feels he is at the centre of it, detached in every way except for the furniture below and in front of him, the diminished bottle of liquor, halved lemons with life squeezed out staring reproachfully at him. It is a fine time to breathe, but there is his head. Doesn't matter where he is, it always travels with him.

The words appear without rippling the setting in any way. 'My first night in Goa was like this Antonio, my son.' Tony turns his head, and there is the Dom, seated on the prow of Dominic's boat, now closer in his vision than the rest, right knee raised to rest an elbow on. This night he looks like the statue at the archaeological museum in Old Goa, all billowing pantaloon, doublet and beard, like Hammurabi, a name Tony loved from his history lessons on the ancients.

'Ay, Dom,' Tony mumbles. 'Long time. How are you?'

'Good, good, borem. What you drinking, men? Caju?' The Dom pinches his nose and makes a face.

'Why, you want? You people bought cashew here, no?'

'Si. And many other things, but that was after my time. How much time I had here? A few months only, no, between sailings and all? Then that bastard disease buggered me so I lie on the ship, with some sailors holding me up to see Goa from—what you call, this thing—Mandovi, for the last time. So lonely. Ungrateful dogs, treating admiral, governor boss of the Estado da India this way. Not good, no, my son?'

'Not good,' Tony agrees. 'I wanted to talk to you, but I didn't know if you had the time...'

'Don't be shy, boy' The Dom's tone suggests disappointment. 'First time we are meeting or *what*, men? How many times we meet since your daddy died? Ten? Fifteen? Silly boy.'

'Who are you calling silly, old man? Vasco da Gama at least has a town to his name. What you got? Nothing! Rua Afonso de Albuquerque is Mahatma Gandhi Road. Praça de Afonso de Albuquerque is Azad Maidan. One ship in your name was there, and that also Indian soldiers destroyed before or after they looted fancy shops, I don't know, when they threw out your people, our people—whatever people. One ship flying Portuguese flag on the bum. Then, boom! Under Mormugao harbour. The end! No *Afonso de Albuquerque*!' Tony draws a finger across his throat. 'Only Afonso bloody mango. A few Afonso here and there and some Albuquerque, maybe thanks to people you did fing-fing with,' Tony uses a made-up phrase from Dino and his childhood.

'Fing-fing?' The Dom appears to ponder on that, as he does on the suggestion that Vasco, no less self-important than he, should have the status of exalted explorer while he that of mere conqueror. Then he decides on a comeback. 'You jealous, son of Francesco?'

'Bastardo!'

'Ah, that I am,' the Dom strokes his beard, slowly, regally, his head turned towards the sea. 'I am that. To do what I did, you have to be a bastard, no? How you conquer so many lands, aanh? You think a wilted flower can walk into Goa and bugger the Idalcão—two-two times—then taking Ormuz, Malacca, what all I did? Estado da India happened because I, Afonso de Albuquerque had the balls and all. Da Gama! Pffft! If I didn't protect his small peppers, he would be nothing, just a sailor boy with big hat. Poof!' Then the wind goes out of his bombast. Deflated, he turns to Tony. 'Why you so angry, baba? What 'appened?'

'Nothing,' Tony mumbles into the glass, switching to a more formal tone from singsong to recall words of the Poet Dantas. 'All I do is wait for the day to end, but now the days never end, my friend. There is so much I cannot tell you, because you may say that would make me less of a…' Then he breaks. 'I don't damn well care any more, Dom, you old fool.'

He should not have said that. Even if they were familiars, and talked like close friends. 'Sorry, boss,' Tony ventures, kicking up sand with his loafers.

'It's okay, my son.'

'Season-time, home thing with Anastasia, Melba-bitch. And again some war Dino is fighting. Sometimes it's all too much. You know what? I'll go to St Catherine's and light some candles. At least it will make you happy.'

It is the wrong thing to remind the Dom of. 'I went there, no? Nothing there. Very sad, all empty. Small church I built for Santa Catarina to give thanks for buggering Idalcão, first day only, killing all those thousands of Moor-type people and writing to the king also, saying I am being good boy for him, Jesu and also his Mrs—not Jesu's Mrs, baba, the *king's* Mrs. And nothing left at Santa Catarina's. Only stone shell—no?—smelling of bat shit. These Dominicans, Franciscans, what big-big cathedrals they have next to my Catarina's home. They had bloody New Year party or *what*, men?'

'You were too famous…'

But it doesn't go any further. Tony will have to wait another day for counsel. The switch is pressed and it is morning. The grey is lighter with the sun still many shades behind.

The boats are coming home fattened with kingfish, sardines and mackerel, maybe some baby shark and ray. The women and children are gathered around near the water. A small girl wears Tony's shoes, clumsily walking on the sand near Dominic's boat, and a boy is running between the palm trees waving the tablecloth like a pennant, noisily chased by other boys and the beach dogs, a happy melee in the pureness of dawn. Zezito stands silently to his right, serenely watching the world go about its business.

The innkeeper stirs himself. It is time to greet his life.

18. The Surprising Seduction of PI Fernandes

'I am like you,' says the Princess. PI Fernandes thinks that is quite clever of the woman.

'I know, we both strongs,' he decides to indulge her. 'We like good tings, no, dehling? And I am good frien'. Very good frien', no? What all I let you do?'

That is true, for the Princess's traffic moves with the smoothness of tides, finding its way through Aparanta's overground-underground.

Fernandes reclines on large floor cushions piled near one wall, which is painted bright yellow, highlighting it against the rest of the room, painted white. Garlands of small blue flowers are painted along each of the two windows, now shut, draped with curtains made from pink-purple-gold saris. Large and small masks brilliantly crafted from leather are behind and above him on the wall, all open-mouthed, hideous with their empty eyes, more so the ones that have cheeks bulging with laughter. The light in the room is from red and blue glass lamps suspended from the ceiling with a slender brass chain. They sway gently with the push from the antique two-bladed fan. The effect is hypnotic. The Princess, her silk robe open in casual repose and invitation, is both creator and enhancer.

PI Fernandes reaches with his hand to push away the embroidered dragonhead over her left breast to reach inside and touch it. He weighs it in his hand. 'So big and heavy-ré,' he inhales. The Princess has class, not like the prostitutes he occasionally blesses in the lock-up, for feely-suck-fuck (not always in that order), before their pimps, or sometimes a persistent and alcoholic brother or husband, arrives to have them released on bail. Recent pickings have been good, as women from Bombay, northern India, and as far away as Nepal and Bangladesh visit in season, adding to an ever-replenished platter.

'A man do what he do, no? Home is home, outside is outside. Remember dat,' he would tell his subordinates, who were sometimes allowed to pick up crumbs after he was done. Excited by the memory, PI Fernandes discovers the right breast of the Princess and squeezes the large nipples on both breasts, which begin to change with his touch, contracting and then releasing a rash of goose pimples in the vicinity.

'You like?' he insists, breathing heavily. 'You like?' This time he squeezes harder and his penis grows painfully, looking to escape his tailored khaki uniform trousers, which always remain with him even as he jettisons his tunic to don appropriate shirts for all manner of engagements.

The Princess continues to look at him, smiling mysteriously, letting his hands wander across her. His head feels a bit heavy. There is incense, and the soft drumming and cymbals from the old-fashioned music system that reaches halfway up the wall with its sleek black components, little wooden birds dangling from various controls on loops of tinsel thread.

'All dis hippie music,' he drawls. Or is it the best of Shiva's kitchen garden? He giggles as he takes another puff from the sheesha loaded with charas. It is conveniently placed by the cushions. The remains of the previous ball of damp tobacco and narcotic are on the ashtray carved out of the belly of a naked brass woman, which PI Fernandes reaches out to caress every now and again.

'All Indu gods, no? Nice hippie-type, like dis ganja-lover god,' PI Fernandes tells the Princess in stream of consciousness, idly dreaming of his fortunes if Shiva were to ever be apprehended in the by-lanes of Anjuna and Vagator—or even Arambol up north— with entertainment drugs. The prodigious blue-skinned god would surely declare these for personal use. And he, PI Fernandes, would threaten to jail him unless he proved generous, in cash and kind.

'Indu gods having fun all times, not like udder gods. Always saying "don't do dis-dat-dat-dat or you going all the way to hell", on bugger National Highway only. Dat's why Indu gods always on T-shirts, and favourite gods of hippie peoples. Good tourist gods.'

The Princess smiles and parts her legs, her crotch still covered with the robe. She is too good, this Brazilian bitch, Fernandes thinks, she even gave him Johnny-boy Black before the sheesha, while she drank wine, urine-pale, like a proper lady. Not so idly, the policeman wonders if he could urge a greater cut from the Princess, who seems to be doing better than he had thought, business must have picked up this past year with the appointment of new couriers and pushers. Fernandes passes the pipe to the Princess, who inhales deeply and lets the smoke slowly curl out and surround the face of the inspector, so they are both wreathed in gently dancing smoke.

'That's not what I meant when I said I am like you,' the Princess murmurs, ignoring the inspector's journey into theology. 'Come, let me touch those...mmmm, not bad.'

'Not bad? *How* you can say? Do you know what all dey see? What dere big brudder see?'

'And where all have they been, hmmm? Come to me,' mouths the Princess, but, instead, goes to him and unbuttons his batik shirt, running her long fingers down his hairy chest and belly, using the nails to work clumps of body hair into swirls and knots like miniature mangroves across the torso. She then gently lowers PI Fernandes's khaki pants, helped by him as he takes the hint and raises his hips so it will be easier. He does a few hip thrusts in the air in joy, escaping from his underwear, and flails the air in front of her face.

'See dehling! See!' PI Fernandes is losing his mind. The one time he forced himself on his wife, Profercia, that way after a few drinks with the boys, she had screamed so loud the children had woken up and neighbours came enquiring. He was forced to come to the door and tell that inquisitive son of a dried bombil Mahesh Gaonkar that his wife had a bad dream and was sick in the toilet—at least that part was the truth. When he had gone back Profercia had been sitting on her knees in front of the squat-toilet like it was an altar, feverishly making signs of the cross. 'Dat's why all dis fancy sex tings are not good at home and all, men,' he would tell his friends at police headquarters with conviction. 'What you wants wife no give or wife no have. Only girlfrien' or randi.'

The Princess swallows him whole and then melts him with her tongue, as she holds down his arms with her strong hands. Too strong, thinks PI Fernandes. He moves his eyes down and notices for the first time her large wrists just before he closes his eyes because the Princess is doing to him things Profercia never would. When he opens his eyes, they are drawn again to her fingers, long and strong, the nails painted violet.

'You have strength of a man, men. Not like our woo-mans, no?' PI Femandes slurs with affection. 'What you eat in Brazil? Beef only, cleant properly and all? Not also fish, pork and chickens?'

The Princess doesn't reply. She reaches for a cut-glass decanter of olive oil, pours some onto PI Fernandes's penis, who keens, nearly insane, as she rubs down the oil. He is wet, and the oil runs past the puckered dip of his anus and onto his lower back as he arches his body again.

'Let me do, let me do, no?' he pleads, but the Princess only smiles and holds down his hands, pinning him in place. He can see her now, naked from the waist up. She shifts, and then she is naked all over. The Princess moves over him and PI Fernandes raises his haunches and says, 'Like dat, aanh? You do like dat, on top?' thinking Profercia would never do it, only lie on her back as he did his man's work.

But something is wrong. The inspector can feel an insistent tapping on his anus and before he can say 'What dat?' it is in him, and he screams in surprise, pain and anger—for the Princess is in him in one smooth motion, as he would sometimes be inside the beggar boys from Karnataka, trash that needed to be treated like trash. Only, he did not use olive oil, just his spit. If they became belligerent, Fernandes would rest his penis and use his baton. 'Tasty, no?' he would taunt the boys, as their eyes bulged. Some would even vomit into their gag or bite their tongues. But those were the raw ones, not the ones with already smooth bum holes, readily open mouths and practised body language from their encounters with tourists, some old enough to be their grandfather and, sometimes, grandmother, though mostly the former.

But now PI Fernandes can't scream even with the pain. The Princess is so strong, weighing herself down on him, that he can't move.

She giggles. 'You like virgins also, no?'

He is paralysed. 'How you…How I…?' he begins to ask, and stops, because the Princess (the Prince?) has chosen that very moment to renew pounding him. Fernandes passes out from the pain and narcotics, with a lasting vision of his shocked penis lying limp across the dense hair of his abdomen, in homage to the power of the man-woman's penis that he can see disappearing into and reappearing from his bum, like a crazed gift with its wrapping of pink condom.

And so it comes to pass that the Princess and PI Fernandes forge a special relationship that night. While he lies unconscious, the Princess calls for Anita, her loyal maid, beautician and occasional lover on lonely days, and asks her to bring in some jasmine and peach tea. As she walks in, Anita sees the inspector cradled in the spoon of the Princess's statuesque body, the sheet a little askew so they are both bare to the elements, their bodies at rest.

The whispers will start in the morning, the Princess knows. Anita will take care of it. The staff will hear it before noon, the village before sunset, all of Bardez by the next day, and all who count in Aparanta before the end of the week. There will be no proof, of course, and nobody will ask—but there will be no need. Word of mouth is the most contagious of diseases, and it will bind PI Fernandes to the Princess more than anything she would pay him for looking the other way. It will also strengthen her position while negotiating with Sergei, for his pretty toy-girls and toy-boys to take their little packets of mind-altering substances to enjoy at Club Havana on the hill overlooking Sodomo, or to take back home, past the tame police in Moscow and Saint Petersburg. Any disobedient Israeli or Nigerian can easily be shooed away.

PI Fernandes will remain her ally through it all, loyal and discreet, or he will disappear, taken by the sea, bound to any of the numerous river beds with weights, or taken to dust in the countless crags and crannies along the coast, feeding all manner of sea or land creatures. His clothes and jewellery will be burnt or buried deep elsewhere, in some backwater in Canacona in the far south, or in a grotto in the dense Sahyadri Hills, deposited there by couriers. The Princess shrugs—isn't that what happens in this crazy world? A few dozen of the unrepentant and foolish disappear each year, like the son of that ambassador from—what was it? Slovenia? Bulgaria? It didn't matter. After a while the newspapers and television people stopped crying in their silly language and then nobody cared any more. But it will not soon come to that, will it? PI Fernandes's surprised anus will heal quickly enough with the thought of enrichment.

Idly playing with her nipples, the Princess recalls a saying of his. 'No time for bad-bad tings in paradise, no?'

19. The Life and Times of Winston Almeida: V

It must be said here: for all the putting the vigorous and increasingly successful Winston did, he longed for love. Indeed, a trophy he could cradle, away from the whorehouses of western India and western Asia; a trophy so respectable that church and society would not crow in dismay. Respect, after all, was a bastard child of wealth.

In the course of business dealings and casual enquiry, Winston thought he had discovered a trophy that combined business and pleasure in Charming de Souza, a lovely widow who ran a successful furniture manufacture and export business. She was alone in the world, her husband, Vasquito, being nearly merged into the asphalt by a truck speeding down the curving slope of Verna plateau as he was crossing the road to ask for assistance to fix his stalled jeep.

Winston thought he wanted Charming, but he was certain he wanted her business. He wished to establish in that space a resort for the growing number of charter tourists, a trend he had identified early on with remarkable prescience as the wave of the future. 'First English and German peoples only, den who-fuck cares *what* peoples if dey have money in bag and bum-pocket.'

He had sent Franklin to enquire, and then Iosif, as Franklin came back rebuffed: 'She said she not selling and "Have a nice day".' Franklin was astounded. 'Is it like two-plus-two is *four*, men… bluddy?' Iosif was offered tea and biscuits but was also sent away with exhortations to have a nice day. Winston then sent his pet sarpanch, Damodar Phadte, with instructions to talk about his great deeds. But Phadte too was sent away with wishes for a nice day and, as a bonus, was asked if Winston wasn't the same gentleman who had slapped his wife outside the church at Varca? A fortnight or so after this last refusal Winston swallowed his pride, gathered his anger, and went to visit the widow.

It was infatuation at first sight, though admittedly one-sided.

Charming de Souza was like no widow Winston had ever seen. Dignified, yet with casual bearing that permitted her to mix freely with workers as she went about urging them to complete orders before the monsoon, or the wood would rot and their bonus trickle into the gutter along with her profits. With her slightly long face set in a head of curls, Charming was redolent of old-world elegance, yet clad in denim jeans and a black T-shirt that reaffirmed her feminine credentials with gusto. On her right breast—left for Winston—was emblazoned the letter D and, after an ampersand, on her left—right for Winston—the letter G. It was all Winston could do to refrain from picking up a saw, noisily and messily decapitating the bloody-men-bugger bhaille workers and ravish Charming right there in the middle of the vast workspace. He would place her on a worktable next to the lathes, cradling in either hand the voluptuous alphabets.

Instead, he opted for the route of a gentleman.

'Hello,' he said. 'Two minutes you have?'

'Two minutes,' allowed the widow Charming, and invited him into her office, a small but efficient space of carved wooden tables and chairs, decorative lampshades and prints advertising the Louvre in Paris and the North Sea Jazz Festival near the Hague. She sat behind a spotless desk, near a rack laden with all manner of books on design and thick files that were variously titled 'Germany', 'UK', 'Italy' and 'Dubai'. She gestured for Winston to sit, who in a fit of uncharacteristic chivalry took his place only after Charming, after first checking for dust on the gleaming chair so his white clothes wouldn't soil.

The widow shrugged and said, 'What do you want?'

'Sister,' Winston ventured, instantly realizing it to be a bad move, as escalation from sibling to paramour would require much work. 'You are knowing me?'

'Of course I know you,' said the widow. 'Who doesn't in this place?'

'Ah, good,' Winston said, relieved. 'Then we are like friends already, no?'

'I am not selling, Mr Almeida. If your visit is about this place, I suggest you leave, as we have nothing to discuss. If on the other hand you're interested in some furniture for your home or your developments, I would be happy to help. Have a nice day.' With that, Charming picked up a yellow pencil from a red-and-black lacquer holder on the desk and impatiently began to tap the unsharpened end on the polished tabletop.

Winston's eyes went red with rage and he began to blink furiously.

'Something in your eye?' the widow enquired solicitously.

'Nutting,' Winston croaked as he wiped his eyes, and wished Iosif and Franklin were by his side. 'I come as friend only and you talks to me like enemy. Why?'

'It's nothing personal, Mr Almeida. This is my life, and it is not for sale.'

Winston was in thrall. Nobody had defied him so openly and with such finality in many years. He discovered he had an erection. He couldn't take his eyes off the magical alphabets on Charming's bosom. He tried another approach. 'You talk to peoples, no? Aks dem, dey tell you I am big developer. Bee-ig. What you get here? So much hard works and den dese Kashmiri peoples hurting local business. Den dese import tings from Malaysia, Indonesia and all. I give you money, cash only, you have good times. You have house near Margao? Dey tell me nice, big place, but lonely, no?'

'No deal, Mr Almeida, I'm sorry. And if you're trying to threaten me, please try your luck elsewhere. Please ask your brothers to stop coming here, along with that slimy sarpanch fellow. This is private property. If you'll please excuse me now, we're busy and there are some orders to finish. My foreman Gopal will show you out. Goodbye, and have a nice day.'

Winston stood up in a huff, realizing that the widow Charming was nearly as tall as he and therefore not a victim to be easily stared down. 'You remember, dis my place. Peoples of dis place want big building here, big hotel for tourists, and Winston Almeida will give big buildings, men, Charming de Souza or no Charming de Souza.' He had stomped off, with the impression that the widow was laughing behind his back.

Charming had not relented, despite the electricity connection being frequently and mysteriously cut off, garbage appearing equally inexplicably in the compound and stocks of teak wood being burnt with acid. A guard mongrel was found dead with its throat cut, and still Charming would not give in. A week later, her foreman could not come to work as a car had swept him from his bicycle. He carried a broken shoulder, mangled hand and shattered knee, a fate that prompted half her workers to desert Charming and leave for their home villages in the faraway provinces of Odisha and Bengal. The remainder she managed to retain with more pay and heartfelt assurances. After a month of nightmares, but not before completing her pending orders with the help of double wages to her workers, purchasing wood with extended credit and requesting help of a second cousin from Vasco strong with transport unions (the local transporters having meanwhile declined to carry her shipments)—the widow retreated to her pretty home in the hills of Margao.

Sensing blood, Winston went after Charming one evening. But it was a poor choice of day, the widow's birthday. It was May-muggy, the air pregnant as if with triplets, the monsoon that would break over Goa to soothe the dryness of the year just weeks away.

Winston drove up the slope to the house with Franklin, Iosif and a carload of burly henchmen, local boys fed on the tried and tested Almeida Bros diet of loot and plunder, flashing gold crucifixes and chains, the accepted currency of success. The lane outside her house, the Villa de Souza, was lined with cars, motor scooters and motorcycles. This had brought forth a frown from Winston: Who would think a widow would have so many friends?

A celebration had begun, and there was loud music, which one of the boys correctly identified as an offering from Sting. But a declaration of 'Ay, Sting-ré, I know, boss' brought only a growled 'Shut up, id-*jut*' from Winston. They marched through the door and a spacious, sparsely furnished all-white living room into the area beyond, a large, open space surrounded by trees of medium height and bushes of tiger lily and hibiscus in many colours. Only the three brothers advanced as, after all, this was still in many ways an exploratory force intent on Winston's brand of diplomacy, not brutal conquest.

Thirty or so guests were milling around a vast carved table laden with drinks, cold cuts, salads and bread. Winston knew nobody and, engaged in completing a ritual, no one paid attention to him. The widow looked dazzling in a white halter-neck and capris, her café-au-lait smoothness so striking that Winston was stopped in his tracks by a familiar feeling of admiration and erection. A man, merely in T-shirt and jeans and leather sandals, was leading others in a toast. It was clear this man and the widow Charming had a special relationship, Winston observed amid the gathering storm in his head, the instinct of an alpha male telling him a worm may have visited intimately the apple of his eye. As Winston watched, the man raised a glass of beer.

'Confusion to our enemies,' he intoned, and the assembled, with raised arms, broke into laughter as they chorused and drank.

The possibility of an acronym flashed through Winston's mind, the briefest acknowledgement of intellect worthy of his hero, but he crushed the thought as he would a sated mosquito. Winston coughed in irritation, and it came out as a deep rumble that precedes a clearing of phlegm. Distracted, the group of people looked his way, and Charming immediately came towards the brothers with two men, one of them formally dressed in a full-sleeve white linen shirt, blue linen trousers and black moccasins, the other the lover, Winston presumed. Widow Charming wore a frown, and Winston wanted again to disarm her and violently disrobe her right there. His erection had become unbearable.

'What are you doing here?' Charming came right up to him, delivered her admonition in frigid tones, her motion moving them all backwards into the living room and away from her guests. She lifted her chin in the general direction of Iosif and Franklin. 'Please take your animals and get out.'

'You say "yes", sister, no?' Iosif tried, scratching under a headscarf patterned with stars and stripes, ignoring her insult.

Charming pretended she hadn't heard him and continued to address Winston. 'If you do not leave now, Mr Almeida, I will call the police,' the widow stood her ground. She gestured at the gentleman in the full-sleeved shirt. 'Oh, I'm sorry, I forgot to introduce you. This is Amitabh Kumar, the new income tax commissioner.'

'You call police? What dey do?' Winston sneered, now beyond reconciliation. 'Arrest me? Putting Winston Almeida in jail? Stupid woo-mans. What will tax-man do, aanh? Not even Goan he is. I know lots-of lots-of peoples in Altinho, peoples who can take dis tax-man and put him back, air freights, non-stop Goa-Delhi tomorrow morning flight only.' He advanced towards her, but the man in the T-shirt glided in to block him.

'What your name?' Winston wanted to kill him.

'My name is Dino Dantas. Stop creating trouble for this lady or you will create trouble for yourself.'

'Tell your mummy bye-bye, Dino Dantas.'

In reply, Dino Dantas, warmed by alcohol and anger, spat on Winston's face.

Winston and his brothers would not forget what happened next. As they rushed the trio—Winston, the widow, and his brothers Dino (the tax commissioner was for the moment too great a risk despite Winston's boast)—two great Doberman pinschers came out of nowhere. One stood on its hind legs, its face inches from Winston's face, the other loosely held Franklin's privates in its jaws, a move that urged Iosif to rapidly backtrack towards the entrance.

'These are police-trained dogs, Mr Almeida,' Charming said, flushed and breathing heavily. They are trained to kill, if it comes to that, those who try to hurt me. If you try this business again, I won't be responsible for what happens. Come on, Donner! Off, boy! Blitzen! Off, girl!'

The giant dogs backed off without a sound and disappeared as miraculously as they had appeared. The brothers retreated as well, shocked into silence, awed by their first public defeat.

On the way back, Iosif had in gentle tones explained the existence of Dino Dantas to Winston. 'Dat Dino, no? He boss of Save Goa…someting. Bluddy bastud-fuck. Always making problems. Stop mining, stop building, stop dis, stop dat-dat-dat.'

Winston Almeida had by now recovered his poise. 'I stop him, no?' he said.

20. An Audience with the Pope

The extraordinary meeting of the board of trustees at Save Goa Society comes to order as it always has, with Founder and Managing Trustee Dionysus Dantas calling to attention the remaining twelve trustees.

They are engaged in desultory conversation around the scarred and ancient tea-stained dining table, at other times the workspace of the general. They are seated uneasily in the small, stifling hot room on hand-me-down chairs, from Ida Dantas's home, Gabru Dantas's chambers in Mapusa and Doctor Benedito's in Margao, and cast-offs from Villa de Vida, courtesy of the innkeeper Tony Calangute, all inadvertent volunteers in Dino's quest.

Incongruous furniture: delicate, carved, high-backed chairs in stolid and stained hewn wood like the table, scratched chairs of modular steel, simple, rusty riveted racks bent from carrying books on law and now burdened by a forest of newspapers, office files and T-shirts with messages. These decorate the two-room apartment. Technology is provided by two ancient computers from the Villa, recycled for the quest. The peeling walls depict art: crayon and colour-pencil dreams of orphans and abused children. The largest is a happy family of stick figures with overlarge heads and lopsided grins. Another has a sun peeking from behind clouds, and a little girl with a smile and flowing tears. This is inspiration for Salvador Dantas. And here he is, among his chosen.

They talk the usual talk. Political compromises by Number One and Co., recent vacations overseas by some of the trustees, investment in land and business and the index of dreams through timely tips. Invitations to address seminars, registers of marriage and hanky-panky, and endless openings of restaurants and tavernas—for this too is a grand pastime in Aparanta, as moths to freebies.

With a spoon Dino taps a glassful of sweet milky tea, brown film already forming on the surface. The chitter-chatter of Aparanta's successful is scythed as one would troublesome monsoon weeds. They freeze, nervous actors aching for the cue.

It is awkward and not entirely unexpected for Dino. It had happened the last time, six months or so previously, when he had called a meeting to brief the chosen about taking his battle to Winston Almeida and all manner of associated vermin. Of course, he hadn't quite expressed it that way, using instead the more politically correct term 'thieving goat-fuck bastards'. In turn, Dino had been warned, in tones better suited to casual conversation and guiding a child, by the Dantas family friend, Brando Gaspar Calisto Pinto, landlord, occasional writer and self-styled pope of Panjim. 'Don't create your own river, Dino. I live by one God created and that is enough for me. I ask you this as an old friend of your family. What are we here for, baba? To build Goa or destroy it? Bad already, no, with bhaille making our lives difficult, taking jobs and all. Now that Goan people want to build Goa in their image, why stop it?'

General Dantas had opted for the facetious to mask a counter-attack. The last time he checked, he told the Pope, bhaille had ruled Aparanta for four hundred and fifty years, and then some other bhaille took over, and now in Aparanta we have nice navy blue Bhaille Republic passports. Unless some of us want nice maroon Bhaille Union passports courtesy of Portugal, evidently a land of bhaille perched like an afterthought on the western seaboard of Europe. 'We also have some nice bhaille names also, no, you and I,' he had beseeched the Pope. Dino had embellished this with a smile and open-palmed supplication. 'We don't have the power to put the goat-fuck thieves in jail, but if we use law and public opinion, we can give them a headache big enough to go back to their mothers, not that any self-respecting mother will accept the goat-fuck swine.'

The Pope, so called after a drunken boast during a harvest festival that with his writings he ruled the Catholics of Aparanta from 'land to Lent', had seemed ready to explode but had not looked away. The others too—when Dino had arced his head from left to right, trapping them variously in moods of shock and surprise, a sprinkle of disgust, a drizzle of fear, perhaps wondering what would befall them if they tangled with Winston and higher powers—had all looked him in the eye.

Today, the Pope has taken his seat at the head of the table to the right of Dino, eyes averted, flicking specks of congealed dirt from the table with a yellowing fingernail. The rest mill around aimlessly, and then in ones and twos seat themselves, none directly in front, but ranged loosely to his left and right. They glance at Dino and quickly look away before he can catch their eye. Even Nita Carvalho, second in command to General Dantas and fellow trustee, seated to his left, leans away as if from a leper and focuses intently on a file in front of her. Indeed, this time the meeting has been invoked by Nita, and she put the phone down on Dino before he had the opportunity to query her. Dino had an inkling, but he wanted confirmation. He had seen all the trustees present as he walked in, not straggling in late as they had for earlier meetings.

'Good morning, friends,' Dino says, craning his neck this way and that, with a sidelong glance at his deputy. She looks smug. This meeting is now old, he realizes. *Now I'm summoned before God, king and judge.*

Dino sits ramrod straight in an attempt to control himself, places his hands palm down on the table, and looks ahead at the wall. It has on it a UNICEF calendar, and he sees the date on it: 2 November. A day before Deepavali. *Shit. I promised to get Anjali* some lanterns and sparklers.

'Good morning, friends,' he again mechanically intones into the silence.

'Is it, Dino, is it?' Immaculada Dias, former calendar girl and Aparanta's emerging activist socialite, asks solicitously. 'Good morning and all?'

Vishwas Parrikar, eminent criminal lawyer, snorts derisively and reaches out for a glass of tea near him, and then stands up to pluck two cream biscuits from the heaped plates at the centre of the table.

'Is it what?' Dino shrugs. 'You need to be clear.'

'No, Dino, it is you who needs to be clear.' That comes from Urmila Naik, chairperson of the Hope Trust for Women and Children and co-trustee there with Immaculada. 'When we call you, you are never there, no? Nita is always there, but she says she does not know what all you are doing. No idea. I only read in newspapers you are going to villages and doing meetings and forcing them to go to court and all.'

'The purpose of Save Goa Society is to create awareness, Dino, my dear,' adds Juliet Martin, inheritor of landed millions and, recently, partner of Vishwas Parrikar at a large beachfront hotel, embroiled in litigation over bypassing zonal regulations. The frail Juliet fingers a string of pearls as Vishwas Parrikar helps himself to more biscuits, making her jump with his scraping of the chair as he rises. Dino reaches out and slides the plate of biscuits towards him. 'Create awareness,' Juliet repeats. 'Nothing more.'

'Those days are over, Julie,' Dino says, looking first at her and then around the table, trying to catch the eyes of the trustees without success. 'Awareness without action is meaningless. Anyway, I didn't start it, did I? I am just reacting to it, trying to prevent things like this from happening in future.' *Look* at me, ye invertebrates, ye complete shits.

'This has nothing to do with us. You are doing this on your

own, Dino. All this land conversion protest and all? Putting cases in high court only?' As Vishwas Parrikar finally speaks, bits of biscuit spray on the table, making Juliet flinch again, and Dino wonders at their compatibility as business partners. 'Did you ask us? Why you give everybody trouble like this? This is not a revolution… like trying to kick out Portugoose…Portuguese people. Now it's a free country.'

'You are taking on too much. No focus…' Balkrishna Desai, clinical psychologist, is perspiring in unaccustomed heat. He uses a large handkerchief to wipe his face. He then snorts into it before returning it to a trouser pocket. 'Save Goa Society should focus on social issues, not also take on environmental issues.'

There is a babble of acquiescent chatter at this and Dino lets it flow around him, his face expressionless, eyes returning to the calendar.

'I have been writing you notes on this for a long time, Dino,' Nita finally speaks, 'but you don't read them.'

Noise of traffic wells up at the busy crossroads below at the crowded enclave of St Inez, in west Panjim, spitting distance, as Dino likes to say, from Altinho. Dino waits for the battle of horns in the crowded mid-morning street outside to quieten before responding, and then turns to look at Nita in a flash, immediately to his left, but her eyes are locked on the file. 'Notes? You need to send me notes when you can tell me any time you wish? For the past two months we have spent days together walking around Goa and discussing plans at home as mummy cooks for us. You need to send me notes? Did you send these notes to the trustees as well?' Dino's laugh comes out as a rasp. Nita is quiet.

◆

'Boredom is the epitaph for too many of us, Dino.' Nita had put out her cigarette in the sand, and then placed the stub in a pouch of her tote bag, pretending she had not seen Dino's approving smile, hesitant though it was with the suddenness and brutality of her statement.

They were at Mandrem, between engagements, moving north from Morjim after attending a meeting at the local community centre, and now on the way north to Harmal—rechristened Paradise Beach by the new wave of hippies and backpackers. The mantle had lain earlier on the Eden-wise sickle-moon of Palolem in the far south, till traveller-litter came to be. Already, others were awaiting the stench of slow death in Utorda, Cabo de Rama and Agonda, Dino told her. Mandrem too. All would in turn be called Paradise Beach in the game of traveller roulette.

'Is this why you think I do this? Because I am bored?' Dino had queried, surprised.

Nita had not answered, only watched him steadily. Dino, inexplicably nervous, had launched into a lecture. Aparanta is a core of a million-and-half people, give or take; a drop in the subcontinent, but an ocean in Aparanta. When we are home, our bellies are filled with pride. When we are not, we do anything to fill ourselves, our pride becoming as fickle as the arrival of the monsoon these days. The numbers keep growing; much of Aparanta is no longer in Aparanta. How many can live off the sea, off the farm? The generosity of itinerants has kept this land fed for generations, fed the myth of self-sufficiency and plenty, ensured several great and lesser houses remain standing, instead of being skeletons of heritage that so often decorate Aparanta's villages and towns, an exhalation away from death. Those that have land, sell to live well for a few years. When that consideration runs out—it ends. Ever more reason for the children of Aparanta to leave. And, in the turn of the coin, ever more reason to stay and take. Many of those who remain see little recourse except the game of public affairs and business by travelling along the easiest route, armed with a compact of fragrant grease. 'We are now like crabs, pulling each other back because we want the mantle of greatness with the least effort. We need to escape from this prison of our own making. We need to grow in less cynical ways.' Dino had exhaled with a loud 'Shih!' A heron stalking the backwaters just behind the tongue of sand they were on, startled by the noise, took flight.

Nita finally broke her silence. 'You have become extreme.'

Dino smiled. 'I guess. It's why I came back here in the first place. There is work to do here, Nita. You know, son-of-the-soil stuff. Tony jokingly calls it "Dino's ambulance service". Hell…'

'I have smaller needs,' Nita had said. She had looked out to the sea—beyond the tiny breakers, there was hardly a ripple in low tide. A line of fisherwomen walked past, wearing green-red saris, all with a comb of bright orange flowers, the aboli crowning neat buns. There was the sea, and nothingness. The fisherwomen were soon past and the narrow road and small huts were across the backwater, too far away to bother with intrusions. Dino lay on his back on the sand, resigned, a straw hat drawn over his face. And Nita had sat by him, a reluctant fellow pilgrim.

Later, they walked along the sands of Harmal. Behind them, from the Church of Our Lady of Vailankanni to the beach, twisting, crowded lanes ran with water leaking from burst pipes, construction sores sprouted, red earth and sewage carving a rivulet through silver-black sand into the sea.

Dino fumed, 'After where we were, this is an abomination.'

Nita had remained silent. Dino suspected something was wrong—she had been quiet too at the meeting they had with a group of villagers—but he carried on regardless, as he was given to do. 'This was once a gem, Nita. You wouldn't know; you haven't been up north that much. Now it's a slum. In time, the slum will move to make way for resorts and villas and the noise of Calangute. The bastards in the panchayats and in Panjim are fighting over who gets how much. Everybody wants to be Mr and Mrs Ten Per Cent, maybe Twenty.'

Dino guided her to the right, a hundred or so yards before passing a stream of effluents from the village and then onto the hillside, passing shacks of bamboo and thatch with fanciful names—Om Bar, Trip with Ganesh Crepe Deli, Reggae Pub, See View, Tato's Tattoos, Mango Shack, Bean Me Up, Third Eye. Then up the gentle slope, winding past more shacks and modest rooming houses and, finally, because the tide was in, a short, steep climb to emerge onto Harmal's secret: a freshwater pool fed by a stream that trickles down the hills, hidden by dense brush and kept from the sea by a curve of sand. It was beautiful and Nita, after inhaling the view, had taken out a small camera, eager to capture life in rectangles.

A small crowd had instantly beset them. 'No pictures, bloody Indian,' heckled one, trying to grab Nita's camera. Dino and Nita had known from the accent he was Israeli, his features not unlike their own. There were others, mostly white.

'This is India, friend,' Dino managed a rare attempt at tact.

'Not here,' another among the knot of ten or so barked. German accent, wearing loose striped pyjamas, a short Rajasthani jacket on his bare torso, head a mass of curls. 'Here not India.'

Nita had finally spoken. 'There is no need to be insulting,' she reasoned. 'What's the problem?'

'The problem is you Indians.' This was a third man, and he edged closer, bringing his circle with him. A girl came into view; to Dino, it seemed as if she were Yael, sometime consort of the karma-laden American Mark from the Villa, but he wasn't sure.

'Why you create trouble, men? Wit camera and all? Fuck off, fuck off.' A voice from the back of the crowd. Intervention from a local. Dino was silent, stunned. He took Nita by her hand; she clutched the camera to her breast. The army, now joined by angry and curious members of other enforcing nations, parted to let them go, but not without jostling them, and with loud suggestions that fucking Indians and fucking Goans should not come to places like Harmal and Anjuna and Little Vagator and Palolem. Indians and Goans should learn when to stay away from India and Goa.

'Come to Goa,' Dino snarled as they began to make their way back, finally free of the pack. 'Come to paradise.'

'Being a paradise is hard work, no?' Nita had suggested weakly, still numb.

Dino grunted in agreement, pleasantly surprised at her attempt at humour after a day spent in near-silence and the disturbing intercept. 'The job description comes with it. This land is beautiful and it's cursed. Today's kings are those who steal from us. This is our heritage, Nita. Velha Goa was built on trade, pillage, religion, ambition and treachery. Nova Goa is no different. Usurpers and thieves walk freely among us.'

Nita had stopped and turned to him then, her eyes troubled, filling Dino with dread. 'People usually have an exalted belief in their goodness, Dino. You should be careful.'

High above them, on rock faces on either side of the lake, two immense faces in coloured chalk continued to watch. On the left was Bob Marley, brooding in yellow, red and green. To the right was Shiva, serene and blue.

'Hijacked saints,' Dino offered, to offset the unease he felt with Nita, '...of the Republic of Freakonia.'

◆

It takes no time for doubt to change to treachery, Dino now knows.

How did they buy you? What did it take? Fear? Money? Or are you doing this because I ticked you off in front of the whole office for making Vijaya, eight months pregnant, walk miles in the sun running your personal errands? Or were you upset that I refused to let you go to Stockholm for a seminar during the biggest awareness campaign in our short and eventful history? Or is it because I refused to loan you money begged from citizens and larger donors, so your husband could buy a sailboat? Who knows, baba? Who the fuck cares any more? Dino still wears his slight smile. I'm so tired I just want to sleep. I'm not Salvador Dantas, like that crazy bastard Professor calls me when he is drunk, just an ordinary man who drowns his confusion and misery in drink. Dear God, I'm so fucking tired. Give me strength, damn you, just a couple of months more. *Stay* with me. Let me stop the bonkmar, then do what the hell you want with me. Just leave my family out of it. Can you do that, you omnipotent, omni-impotent...oh, forget it.

'There's talk you drink too much.' Dino silently acknowledges Balkrishna Desai: Yes, I do, you headfuck. 'It could be clouding, no, your judgement? Also, personal problems, could be.' Parrikar nods emphatically to Balkrishna Desai's prognosis, reaching for more biscuits.

Dino is counting. Five trustees haven't spoken yet, not counting the Pope, but he has abundantly made his point.

The silent quintet are Augustus Cotta, retired secretary of welfare, stiff in his crisp white shirt and linen suit; Shashikala Madgavkar, chairperson of Aparanta's Destitute Homes, in jet-black sari, a decorative chopstick inserted into the silver bun at her nape; Avertano Noronha, upstanding leader of the local travel agents' association, resplendent in batik; ever-large Expectacao Alvares, heritage conservationist; and sparrow-like Edwina D'Cruz, famed organizer of Christmas charities, frugal in her frock tailored at the tiny Lisbon Fancy Store at Panjim's Church Square.

The Pope finally speaks. 'You think this is a joke, Dino?' His eyes are elsewhere. He scratches his cheek, in the same motion flicking specks of dandruff from his sideburns. Juliet sees that and crinkles her lips.

'Uncle Brando, do you *know* what is going on in north Goa and other places?'

'It is over, Dino. Either you stop, or we will be forced to make you stop. We all feel it is for the best.'

'How much have they paid you, Uncle Brando? Or have they threatened you? A piece of illegally extended farmland or a little fing-fing on the side?' He looks directly at the Pope.

'I think this is all quite pointless, Dino.' The Pope is flushed. 'I was hoping you would see sense after the last meeting. I even had a word with Gabru to put some sense into that head of yours—either he hasn't, or you're a fool, and that is clear from the rubbish you speak, like a little boy only.' The Pope then looks around the table, frowning briefly at Vishwas Parrikar, who continues to devour cream biscuits, noisily crushing the circular things, flecks of orange cream now added to the crumbs on his moustache. 'I propose that Nita Carvalho immediately assume directorship of Save Goa Society.'

'And I second it,' Immaculada is pleased to contribute. She uses a fingernail to collect the brown film formed over the tea and flicks it into a corner of the room. Juliet looks ready to rub Immaculada's nose in it.

'Those in favour, please raise your hands,' the Pope announces.

They all do. And still they won't look at Dino.

Then the Pope passes judgement. 'This is better for all of us, I think?'

But Dino is away, talking to himself, repeating a chant over and over again, a whisper that builds in pitch. He rocks gently as he says it. The apostles look at each other, and then at their deposed prophet, his lowered face masked by his long hair.

'What is it, my boy?' The Pope is solicitous in victory.

They can hear it now. 'Pobresa, Humidade, Obediencia.' Over and over. Poverty, Humility, Obedience. Dino slowly looks up and into the eyes of the Pope. 'Remember the writing on the wall, uncle? Below the image of Christ in the Cathedral of St Francis of Assisi in Velha Goa. You pointed it out to us those many years ago, remember? Tony and I? Pobresa, Humidade, Obediencia. The mantra of the world. You said that to two teenage boys. Cleans the tabernacle of innocence better than the best detergent. You said that.' Dino begins to jab his forefinger at the Pope. '*You* said that, dammit.' Dino is shouting.

'Dino, you have gone mad!' the Pope thunders, agitated, and looks around for support. 'This…'

Dino inhales deeply, calming himself. 'This apartment belongs to Ida Dantas. She has leased it for free to Save Goa Society, as you are aware,' Dino states formally. 'That will soon cease. And given the exceptional nature of your action, I will be constrained to serve you with legal notice.' Dino rubs his forehead.

'It was good while it lasted,' he says quietly. 'Would you all please go away now?'

They turn to look at him in surprise, but as Salvador Dantas is looking down, he misses this small victory. After a few moments, it is he who leaves, without looking anyone in the eye, but with a lasting image of Vishwas Parrikar's hand frozen over the depleted plate of biscuits, like a greedy altar boy.

21. And a Little Bit of Closure

It is the same day, the day before the homecoming of heroes, and Tony, seated in his office, has a vision. Joanna's head is tilted and it is as if her ears have grown, extended like the honeysuckle speaker of a gramophone. Dino sits in front of that ear like the faithful dog on the labels from Francesco's old 78 rpm records of opera and tango, telling Joanna how much he likes her legs, when all Joanna wants to do is listen to how Dino will make good use of them, intertwining his in hers for a bout as masonry-shaking as the rutting of Melba. What a pair they would make.

'You listening?' Dino nudges Tony with the toe of a sandal. 'And why are you grunting like a pig, Tony Calangute? Ah, Joanna darling, you look lovely. Any time you want to leave patrao and come to me you can come, okay? We'll get married, have six children and fight every day. My Anjali will be the big sister. What do you have here? Just this hotel boy getting fat on tourist money and ordering you around.' Joanna, the reservation clerk, giggles, as she does whenever Dino tells her anything.

Tony signs the papers Joanna brings to the office, bills to be paid for provisions and liquor, refund for a guest who had to cancel a reservation, a handwritten note from Janardan Naik saying he wants to bring the family to dinner on his birthday the following weekend. Tony's gift will be the dinner, he knows, because the chameleon-fucker thief picks a new place to eat from Sodomo to Calangute every other day. Tony tells Joanna to call the sarpanch and let him know all tables are reserved for the season and let him go jump into Sodomo Creek if he doesn't like it. Joanna giggles at that, and Dino looks surprised—this is more his approach. She leaves with a lingering look at Dino. To Tony it seems she would be willing to work on the first of their six at that moment. Dino, adept at playing to the gallery, blows her a kiss.

Tony cannot resist admonition. 'Why are you giving her a hard time, men?'

'Lovely.' Dino leans back on Francesco's chair. 'Why are you so tense?'

Tony ignores the question. 'Let it be, Dino, okay?' he says instead. 'Everything will be fine again.'

'I'm letting everything be, brother mine. I have all the time in the world now to let things be. I have to go see Anjali. I promised to take her out.'

Dino stops by the door. He has something to say, Tony knows; so does he, but he will first hear from Dino.

'What happened?'

'The bastards got rid of me. Uncle Brando was the ringleader, can you believe it?' Tony sees Dino's hands trembling. 'I knew they would try something, but this...I'll start something else. I'll ask mummy, I'll ask Charming, Tilly...will you help?' He looks up, a lost child. He is playing with fire, Tony tells him. He should think with his head, slow down. But Dino is beyond listening. He begins to open the door.

Tony too will not be stopped. 'That MB came over in the morning...almost threatened Umesh when he tried to stop him from entering the office. I tried to call you but the phone in your office was busy...Why don't you carry a bloody cell phone?' Tony looks away.

'Go on. Say it.'

'He said he would offer prayers...'

'He can offer prayers whenever he wants,' Dino brushes his hair back with both hands, smirking, recovered a little from his grief. 'Doesn't he, five times a day?'

'*You!*' Tony shouts, sick with fear. 'You fool-bastard. He said he would offer prayers for *you*!'

◆

'Is that why you drink so much?' Anjali asks, 'Because you miss mummy?'

'No darling,' Dino is quick to reply. Too quick, he thinks to himself. 'I have you, no? But I miss having a grown-up friend. Grown-ups need friends too.'

'Are you going to marry Tilly-mummy—Tilly-aunty—then?'

'I've only just met her, baby girl,' Dino smiles at the directness of the question, and ruffles Anjali's hair. She leans towards him.

'Then I will have three mummys, Granny-mummy, Nasty-mummy and…'

'Yes,' Dino cuts in, 'now finish your ice cream.' He ruffles her hair again—Anjali still hates that, he sees, as she draws back. God, but it's been a long time, too long in his anger-madness for time with Anjali. Nothing like a kick in the bum to bring out paternal sentiments, Dino smiles to himself.

'Are you going to marry her?' Anjali misreads the smile. 'I saw you kissing in the car, no, yesterday, when you took her back?'

Dino chokes on his beer. Anjali laughs and claps her hands. 'Yes, yes, yes! Dino-daddy and Tilly-mummy!'

'Be quiet,' Dino, flushing, gives her a fierce hug. They sit that way, clinging to each other, oblivious of the stares on Sodomo beach. To Dino the sun looks like the yolk of a country egg, red-orange. In a few minutes magic will adopt this berserk ball of fire and turn it into poetry. Sunset. When did I last see one?

'Nasty-mummy says you get angry because people do bad things.'

'Yes, very bad things.'

'Like the blood-gun people on TV?'

'Where did you learn that?'

Anjali ignores the question. 'But you don't have a gun, no? How will you fight with them?'

'You don't worry, baby girl.'

'But you are always getting a little bit angry. *Why*, no? If you didn't get angry and drink so much we could do this more...'

'Yes.'

The sun is finally swallowed by the water, restless in mid-tide, though it remains as a memory.

'Look at this place, Dino-daddy. It's so full of nature, no?'

Anjali is telling him how they will go home and light paper lanterns. Dino nods absently. And unto thee I commend myself, thou dysfunctional God person. If thou permitest anyone to hurt her, do anything to my people, I shall personally undertake a war to ban thee from all imagination. I shall... Dino Dantas sits there with tears streaming down his face, tears that Anjali at first does not see as she is still feeding on the sunset and the waves breaking on the shore with the impending tide. When she does, caught by Dino-daddy's intake of breath that ends in a racking sob, she reaches up to wipe his tears, puts her arms around his waist and cradles him, and General Dantas allows an age of anger and grief to pour from him.

22. The Life and Times of Winston Almeida: VI

It was a day when movement and sound were suppressed with the heavy, moist air of monsoon-in-a-moment. The poetically inclined chief secretary of Aparanta would later the same evening, over cocktails, tell MJ that it had been so quiet on Altinho 'you could hear a lotus bloom'.

MJ was struck by the beauty of the chief secretary's words, a lady otherwise not widely known for flourishes beyond signing her name in red on documents in acquiescence, and in green on every document in negation, as if to unsettle those conditioned to expect the opposite of these colours. He had delicately touched a monogrammed handkerchief to his brow, moist even in the charged air-conditioning of the sprawling waterfront hotel in Miramar, down the tree-lined avenue from Panjim, and added his own wisdom—to him, pearls before this outsider-swine.

'Ah, yes,' MJ had trilled, sipping a sweet red from Douro in fair Portugal. 'Ah, yes. It is a time when everybody and everything open their doors to welcome the light.'

The chief secretary, diplomatic instinct honed in the years spent with Number Ones and lesser numbers, smiled in appreciation. Inwardly, she thought MJ's dalliance with houseboys, which was as much a secret as saying usury follows greed, had robbed him of his faculty. And the wine, his copious drinking of which was as much a secret as saying greed follows usury, had made a soak pit of MJ's head.

But we digress. This was also the day when Winston Almeida of

Varca, heir to Olimpio and to history, was finally called to audience with Number One, helped in no small measure by Vimochan Sardessai. It was a measure of one good Brahmin connecting a potential partner from the lower gene pools to another good Brahmin—mythical stock distilled twice in the unequal game of creation, like feni, as it were.

Aware of such undercurrents, the ever-practical Winston had entreated Iosif and Franklin at a pre-summit meeting, '*How* it matters where my father came from, sorry-men, *our* father, may his soul rest in peace?' He had rightly dismissed such prejudice for the cause of shareholders and stakeholders of Almeida Bros. Any humiliation was worth a seminal visit to Altinho. It was a seat of power so exalted that the Bishop, Dom Afonso's seedlings, the Portuguese consul, the army commandant, the chief secretary and her underlings, and sundry brokers of might and wealth, were all resident on the hill.

'One day, I will own house here, no?' Winston silently promised himself as he was driven in his new car, coloured a shiny gold with seats upholstered in the best zebra-striped velour Goa had to offer. The Korean luxury sedan had been earlier earmarked for a garbage clearance contractor from the once charming town of Margao, a politically connected man who also moonlighted as a slumlord. Winston had jumped the queue, and the car was made his by the simple process of having Franklin telephone the Indian manager of the automobile dealership and assert that Winston would take only a gold-coloured car, not the blue powder puff he was being offered. If the pre-eminent son of the soil did not receive the car by the end of the week, who could tell what would happen to the cars parked in the dealer's impressive lot on the plateau of Verna? The phone call had set in motion a chain of events that included the Korean factory manager in faraway Madras, his boss, and a hurried conference call with their hapless representative in Aparanta to check the tyre pressure, so to speak, of Mr Almeida. When the reading came back, certifying that Winston had enough to cushion him against most potholes, the executives collectively and prudently decided to ignore the slumlord. (Again, we digress. But it is important to establish the parameters for a first meeting with Number One, as accoutrements of show, much like the outrageously flamboyant display feathers of a peacock in pre-rain glee, are important components of such meetings. At home, where he kept his mistress, Felicidade, Winston's overt display when he entertained comprised—besides the deep back of Filly-dehling's evening dress and swooping decolletage—a showcase containing Johnnies Red, Green, Black, Gold and Blue. But that wouldn't do for a first meeting with Number One, would it? And so, the car.)

◆

As Winston made his way up the hill, the man he was to meet, the patrao of all Aparanta, was readying himself. The true patrao, as he ceaselessly reminded courtiers, not the man who held the hollow title of governor and lived a life of luxury on the Cabo, the tip of land close to the ravaged concrete hillsides of Dona Paula, travelling in fancy cars, getting in the way of government business and traffic.

'So you have found another bakra?' Number One asked his trusted lieutenant Vimochan Sardessai.

'Not bakra, saib,' Vimochan Sardessai was quick to point out the economic status of the sacrificial goat. 'Wealthy bakra.'

'Some influence among RC people also, isn't it? You told me he would be no factor in the by-elections, but he went ahead and got that son of a sheep the seat in Benaulim.'

True to his proud Hindu lineage, Number One would protect the quadruped more suited to his sensibilities—the goat—as sheep delivered meat of stronger smell. Besides, he thought sheep to be the favourite of Roman Catholics and Muslims, who he felt were getting in the way of Goa's true future, in the same way many of his party bosses felt all manner of Christians and Muslims with their proselytizing ways were getting in the way of a proud Hindu nation. He shared his deepest sentiments with like-minded intellectuals of Aparanta in broken English, for he was loathe to speak Portuguese, to him a tongue that reeked of colonialism. But English was acceptable, the 'No. 1 language in the world' he liked to say. And who was he to object if that particular colonial tongue had knit the stressed provinces of India as intimately as instruments of governance?

'I was wrong.' Vimochan Sardessai wisely refrained from pointing out to his boss that it was Number One's own reluctance to trust Winston Almeida that had brought electoral defeat to their door. 'The son of a sheep', a former Number One, an RC with no such problems, had benefitted from Winston's support and won a seat in the assembly of Aparanta—and had therefore taken one away from the nervous coalition of Number One. This development had brought about the meeting, as much as entreaties of Vimochan Sardessai to meet the redoubtable Winston. However, Vimochan Sardessai, twice born and, many said, thus twice blessed with wisdom, was a politician's politician; he made it appear that meeting Winston had been Number One's idea all along. 'You are right to cultivate this man. It will bring us much benefit.'

'Benefit, aanh, Vimochan-bab? The usual way?' queried Number One. He took pride in his sense of humour.

'Offshore,' Sardessai switched from Konknni to English, discreet with his reference, one never knew these days who or what lurked behind walls. Offshore was wise, for only foolish leaders of people would keep money near them. Safe havens could be legitimately reached, through an official tour to promote the beauty of Aparanta; or to inspect municipal plumbing preferably in the Caribbean, also recipient of much rain, to ensure roads in Aparanta did not flood during the monsoon; or to renew cultural links with the sons and daughters of Aparanta now scattered across the world in the UK, Dubai, Australia, Canada...

'I know what we want from him.' Number One interrupted Vimochan Sardessai's brief reverie. 'What does this RC friend of yours want?'

'Not much,' said Vimochan Sardessai. 'Right now he is just looking at some land north of Chapora, coastal land.'

'Not much? How much?'

'A thousand acres or so. Here and there. To begin with, then much more. Maybe two thousand. For now.'

'He might as well buy a taluka.'

'He and some friends of his. Some Russian friends.'

This jolted Number One from his studied nonchalance. His nearly absent eyebrows twitched in enquiry. Then he sat up straight, grim.

'They are already here, sir,' Vimochan Sardessai hurriedly explained. 'You get the reports, you know what they contain. It's the same with some of those traders and travel agents who give refuge to terrorists and launder drug money. Let Delhi worry about security threats, na? Why should we stop plucking mangoes when they are ripe?'

Number One smiled at that. His deputy had a way with words. He also had a way with plucking mangoes, if reports from Aparanta's intelligence bureau were to be believed. But what man did not feel the need to pluck mangoes from a young and attractive orchard now and again?

'If we tracked down everyone who breaks the law, the economy would disappear,' Number One allowed Vimochan Sardessai to continue. 'We would have rioting on our hands and less funds. Now the balance is not perfect, but at least it is there. Drugs are mostly being used by tourists, let them destroy themselves, how does it matter? If there is a fight for territory, gangs will finish each other off—I don't think too many locals will be affected except those directly involved in the trade. It's fine as long as every now and then we put some small goonda in jail to keep the public happy.'

'So you think this Almeida and these Russians can be controlled?' Number One wanted to be certain.

'Most businessmen want to control politicians, sir. With the economy doing better, they forget we also have the freedom of choice.'

At that, for truer words were not spoken that day, Number One and his trusted deputy shared laughter. When they had settled, Number One's personal assistant called to say Winston Almeida had arrived with his brother, Iosif.

'Yusuf?' Number One was immensely irritated.

'No, saib. Iosif. I-O-S...'

'Okay, okay,' Number One dismissed him and turned to Vimochan Sardessai. 'What kind of name is Iosif?'

◆

Number One walked around the large mahogany desk towards Winston with outstretched right arm, while Vimochan Sardessai got up from his visitors' chair, the fifth and last in the arc that ended to the right of the table, below a portrait of the first Number One of Aparanta. Portraits of successive Number Ones were displayed across the walls, with a break for the President of India, and Number One's spiritual leader, a gentleman who deeply believed that anyone who ate cow would be present for all eternity at the table of Yama, the God of Death, a monumental spear up his anus and out somewhere near the neck, slowly roasting along with all others who decried the virtue of this divine quadruped. Number One took pleasure in administering empire in full view of these worthies, knowing they could do little except to impotently stare.

'Come, come, no?' Number One expansively greeted Winston. He had decided to conduct the interview in English, forsaking both Konknni and Marathi, the two tongues that battled for supremacy in Aparanta while English gratefully seeped in.

Winston was pleasantly surprised at the warmth of the tone and vigorously shook Number One's hand, smiling broadly. Iosif was, for this important day, wearing a bandana with the colours of Portugal's football team, the large swathe of maroon and strips of green providing exuberant counterpoint to his all-black suit. In his excitement at finally meeting Number One, and realizing with shock that the really powerful did not need to display power with conspicuous cars and clothes, Iosif squeezed the hand of Number One hard enough for the diminutive man in a simple blue shirt and tan trousers to wince and lose composure.

'Sorry boss,' Iosif apologized to Number One, without realizing the loss of face he had caused the man his brother had come to do business with.

Winston, more attuned to such niceties through his copious reading of self-help books by his namesake, began to blink rapidly. Vimochan Sardessai, directly across from Winston, nervously counted the moments before Winston's eyes would go red and begin to water. He belatedly accepted that he ought to have briefed Number One more fully—besides ensuring that Winston's faeces-eating pig brother stayed by the car, dusting it or whatever underling brothers did as they waited. Now the inevitable happened, and Winston's eyes began their dance of anger-madness. It fascinated Number One, and he made a mental note to ask Vimochan Sardessai later if the thug was diseased, in which case they would need to rework their strategy. For the moment, however, Number One saw an opportunity to exploit weakness and recover some pride destroyed by the thug's sibling.

'All is okay? Something in your eye only?' he asked Winston solicitously. 'No problem, no?'

'Yes, no?' Winston mumbled, a little confused, deeply wishing he could send Iosif on a terminal journey, like Iosif's namesake had done to several million good Soviet citizens with barely a twitch of bristly moustache. However, typically, Winston recovered with fortitude and said, 'Tank you, no?' determined to make up for what Iosif lacked in social grace.

'Yes, yes,' Number One brushed it away. 'Come, we all sit on the sofa. More better.'

Number One was feeling good, having seized control of the meeting. He politely seated his guests and then sat himself. 'I am hearing lots-of about you. So tell us, Mr Almeida, *what* your secret of success is?' With a wink to Sardessai he added, 'Like we say, mantra, no?'

'Dis dat,' Winston casually offered in an attempt to get back into the contest, willing calm with a wave of his hand. 'Dat dis.'

He then decided to press this minor recovery, examined his fingers as if they belonged to someone else and disdainfully looked around the room. It was painted a pallid ochre, bereft of any decoration except a calendar and the portraits on the wall, and, on the table, a framed photograph of India's Prime Number, a mild man in a turban. He was Number One's professed political opponent from another party—but a generally honourable man, Number One admitted freely, even to Winston when he caught the thug looking at the photograph.

'Good, good,' said Number One, still humouring Winston. 'Vimochan-bab has been telling about your plans. They are big plans, Almeida. Some say too big. It has issues not on the agenda of the productivity council of GGCCII, isn't it? No minutes only, no?'

Vimochan Sardessai took the cue and laughed politely at Number One's joke. Winston managed a smile, but Iosif, being obtuse, laughed louder than warranted and congratulated Number One with a look all around: 'Good one, no, boss?'

Winston decided Iosif would require corrective surgery. Perhaps his penis would need to go. It might look nice placed in the pig's mouth and, if it didn't, at least it would keep him quiet. For the moment, Winston was able to pulverize that thought as he had taken to pulverizing red ants that always tracked him as he ate, eager for the bits and pieces of animal and cereal the great leader sprayed with his feasting. To counter further loss of face, Winston rapidly outlined his plan. 'If you not tinks big, no, how you can win the war?'

'A strategist, aanh?' Number One said indulgently. And, as his deputy had briefed him about Winston's inspirational fetish, he added, 'Like Churchill only. Sweat and tears, no?'

'Blood also,' Winston gravely clarified, pleased to be finally dealing with a politician, Indu bugger or not, who was acquainted with true heroes. 'Blood also.'

'And cigar? Cigar also?'

Now Winston was really pleased. Beaming in appreciation, he decided to display knowledge about global affairs to gain Number One's respect. 'Cigar now only for—dis ting—White House peoples liking blue dress. And termite…minate…uh, acting peoples wanting to be White House peoples only, no?'

The repartee brought forth a gale of laughter from Number One and in that instant Winston was assured of his place in the history of Aparanta. 'What you want, Almeida? You want tea? Vimochan-bab, please give tinkle to office for tea. We have wine biscuit from Loutolim also. Good RC—uh, good tasting.'

That out of the way, Number One resumed business. 'Two thousand acres you want, beginning only? But that is lot, no? He is telling, later you want more also. How much work this poor Vimochan-bab will do, talking-talking to everyone?'

'Many ways to talk, no?' Winston offered. 'I am reading in American book, dey say one good ting, big ting, in all ting of lifes.' Winston paused for effect. He dearly wished he had his guru's prop of tobacco, but in the absence of cigars, he felt that getting to his feet and thereby imposing his impressive height on Number One would be appropriate. So he stood.

'Money talking, no?' Winston towered over Number One. 'Why dese buggers not give, men—sir—if money talking, talking lots-of also?'

'That is why I am in politics and you are in business, Winston-bab. Sardessai will explain method,' Number One figuratively sliced Winston's legs below the knees, forcing him to resume his place with a loud thump.

'This not Salcette, Winston-bab, like your own bathtub—you have bathtub at home, no, with jakuji? And gold tap?' Number One paused here to allow his reach of information to sink in. 'You tell to your foreigner friends: if any trouble, it is finish. Files and rubber stamp will finish. Everything very much quiet, understand?'

'Yes, sir,' Winston said, and Iosif looked at him in surprise, as Winston only ever referred to two people as 'sir'. One was the flower-eared Olimpio, and the other, his namesake.

'How long this is taking, Sardessai?'

'Two years maximum for all land conversions, buying, construction, sale and all. If we help.'

'Okay,' commanded Number One. 'Y'all making plans. Keep me in the loop. Achcha, what is arithmetic, Sardessai?'

Winston had been waiting for this. 'Ten?'

'Ay Winston-bab, these Planning Commission peoples always telling me "plan for inflation-ré". Big balloon, baba, going *up* only, no?'

'Fifteen?'

'Hmmm. Talk to Sardessai. All as usual, Vimochan-bab?'

Vimochan Sardessai nodded in agreement, relieved the conversation was finally on the national highway instead of some insignificant village by-lane.

'Okay, thank you, thanks. Keep me informed—time to time only, okay?' Number One said by way of dismissal, with a sternly wagging forefinger, and started to walk back to his desk. He had to prepare for another meeting afterwards, with the Number One who had preceded him. This would be over convivial luncheon at a discreet table at Martin's Beach Corner on the southern coast. The deal would be done in the best tradition of Number Ones: to protect various improprieties of the predecessor. So, if an incumbent Number One were to become a predecessor by a quirk of fate— either betrayal of legislators or a firmly planted kick on the bum by a livid electorate—tradition would ensure successive Number Ones too would be amenable to accommodation. Number Ones as a tribe were well versed in the theory and practice of protectionism.

Winston had one more thing to say, and he did so with supreme confidence.

'Sir, one ting only,' he announced.

Number One stopped in mid-stride, shoulders tensing with irritation.

'Dere is dis problem, no? Dis...NGO peoples. Always putting stop sign on business, all type business, making traffic jam and all, much badder than Panjim in rushing hour.'

'*Who* dat?' Number One had turned around, and then checked himself when he realized he had adopted the RC's intonation. 'Who that is?' he enquired again, crossly.

'Dino Dantas. Saligao boy, running NGO, Save Goa someting. *What*, no, Iosif?'

'Society. Save Goa Society,' Iosif said, pleased to be finally included.

'Yes, yes,' Number One offered gruffly, for he too had been a victim of Dino Dantas's campaigns. Even a veiled threat to have his organization's papers examined hadn't been enough to banish this meddling Dantas. 'You do what you have to do only, Winston-bab, you understand?' Number One said in judgement, with a deadpan expression and not even a wag of forefinger.

Winston, who had for the first time witnessed a Number One taking such decisions, was speechless with respect at how much could be conveyed with such little effort. 'NGO people are not all Goa,' Number One continued. 'Give this NGO people some discount with this thing, that thing—house, holiday, think of something, no? You do that, this Dino will become devil from god. No need to convert people like olden times, Winston-bab. Today this Increase…Inquiz…this thing…is done with money and power, not God and torture. If this also not stop that Dantas boy, then…' Number One shrugged.

Winston nodded. But he wanted to have the last word in this meeting, so it would leave an indelible impression. He picked up a glass of water from the four that had lain untouched through the meeting.

'A toast…' he requested.

'Okay, okay,' Number One agreed, as he, Vimochan Sardessai and the awed Iosif raised their glasses of water bottled from one of the few Goan springs that remained.

'CTOE,' said Winston, his tone sombre, unmindful of ironies, pleased to have learnt a lesson from even the hated Dantas, for Winston was wise and he took his guidance from wherever it came. That lesson had cost him nothing except a little loss of face, ruined chances of putting the widow Charming and briefly slowed his empire-building.

Iosif stepped into the breach, loyal as ever. 'Confusion to our enemies, no?'

23. Ida Gets a Tip from Highly Placed Sources

Late in the day of the homecoming of heroes, after a spell of surprising rain caresses Aparanta, after he helps Anjali and Ida light Casa Esperança in a profusion of paper lanterns and love, Dionysus Dantas is introduced to the rest of his life. Tilly is with him to witness it.

Tilly will in a few hours, when she finally reaches the Dantas residence in Saligao with the help of Bing and Ujjwala, friends Dino had taken her to meet in the village of Tivim, be comforted by Ida and then quizzed by her. Later, Ida will go to her room to have a little chat with the Mummy of the Son of God, leaving Gabru to talk to these friends, and emerge a little before dawn to go directly to Tilly, whose tears will by then have dried. She will sit by Tilly's side on the settee of carved wood and faded brocade, hold the lover of her child and rock her as if she were her own. She will tell Tilly that she knows, because she has been provided a tip by a highly placed source, that Dino will not be coming home. The police have been told, so the household can only wait for news, or the sun, whichever comes first.

Meanwhile, Dino Dantas's date with the Fates is going astoundingly well—depending, of course, on the point of view.

◆

To review: Dino and Tilly are at the charming, rustic house of Bing and Ujjwala, drinking joy. Alongside, they feed variously on news of the coup at Save Goa Society, a play at the University of

Goa on Nelson Mandela's incarceration at Robben Island prison, and thin strips of beef made tender in lemon juice and then stir-fried—a recipe brought by Bing & Fly on their return from Dar es Salaam across the ocean. Where they sit on the balcao, light from Chinese paper lanterns play over them as they sway in the breeze. The lanterns light up this house as they do all Aparanta for a few days, beacons of hope and prosperity. They light up Villa de Vida, the Casas Serena and Esperança, the grand houses of Number One, Winston Almeida, Vimochan Sardessai, PI Fernandes, the Princess, Sergei Yurlov, even the façade of MB's Boom Shack. Pieces of string, coloured paper and light glued together in magical globalization.

As Dino and Tilly drive home in Dino's trusty Fiat, two large cars with darkened windows begin to follow them as soon as they turn onto the main road to Mapusa, which they must take to reach Saligao. But our new lovers are too euphoric with the evening to pay attention.

The cars travel sedately in inadvertent convoy past the rain-soaked village through a forest of steam that rises from a wet road still scorched from the sun. There is only one irritation: the headlights of the car behind that glare into the rear-view mirror of Dino's low car. It causes him to silently enquire of St Christopher, as they pass the church of the patron saint of travellers, if these people are driving their mother's bum. Just past St Christopher's, as the road rears up to plateau from a curving dip, the headlights overtake Tilly and Dino, form into a car, and then another, and then into a blockade with a screeching of tyres. This forces Dino, who has forgotten to wear his seat belt, to strike his lips on the steering wheel and bleed a modest cut. Tilly, better trussed, is merely jolted.

The explanation comes quickly, without a word being spoken. In the lampless dark—for the roads of Aparanta are rarely lit, almost never when it has rained—shapes emerge. They open the door on

Dino's side and two robust arms reach in to drag him out before he or Tilly can say a word. When Tilly does let out a scream, in surprise and rage, of universal, impotent queries at such times—'Who are you? Why are you doing this?'—the episode ends as quickly as it began, with Dino being savagely hit on the side of his head and then dragged by two men to the large car, a dark-coloured SUV. Tilly sees by the car a flash of patterned white shirt and wonders where she has seen it before. A third man holds her by her arms. He reaches into the pockets of her jeans and then squeezes her breasts before pushing her violently. She staggers back towards the Fiat to land on her back and sees the brute holding her mobile phone. When she screams Dino's name, it doesn't matter, because there is nobody to hear her.

Perhaps minutes pass, perhaps days. Tilly finally collects herself and trudges the angry, fearful, empty distance through quietened Tivim, to the home of Bing and Ujjwala. Dino's dented chariot has disappeared with him, and Tilly is again alone in the world.

24. Dionysus Dantas's Date with the Fates

Dionysus the Learned knows of the Fates of the ancients. As night wears on, he is reacquainted with them and their hangers-on. It is a full night at the Princess's lair.

Sergei Yurlov is Clotho, the spinner, for he makes the world go round and has decided upon the demise of Dino the same as he must the demise of all those who presume to intrude into the Great Game. The Princess assumes the role of Lachesis, for it is she who has picked Dino from among a score of unbelievers in the art of trance as the person most likely to jostle her paradise, and so she is the drawer of lots. The worshipper of the First Sea Lord, Winston of Almeida Bros, whistles tonight for Dino a final, rigged offside signal before the end of the game to prevent the opposition from scoring. So he is Atropos, because life must inevitably draw to a close and Winston has sworn on the spirit of Winston the Elder that while the Dantas pest might win a battle or two, Winston the Younger shall win the war. (The gender business with regard to the Fates, drawing parallels of female forms with male ones, is irrelevant, the Princess having in any case confused the issue.)

As Dino, on his knees, opens his eyes after the blindfold is removed and then the gag he first sees the Fates, directly in front of him seated on elegant, high-backed cane chairs. Then he sees their associates, some standing, some seated on smaller chairs and large floor cushions. There are Winston's two brothers whom he last encountered at the widow Charming's. Iosif is wearing a black headscarf, a sign of mourning, as Iosif is always considerate to his conscience, driven by nagging fear that sometime, somewhere, the carpenter's gifted son will ambush him. Franklin pensively eyes Dino, and then, ever the gentleman, offers a cream-silk handkerchief to wipe the blood off Dino's mouth. But Dino shrugs away the gesture. He sees PI Fernandes, half in plainclothes, wearing a loose white shirt with elegant black cranes on it, smiling at him, and MB, too, scowling, stroking his sharply clipped beard. Dino notices the underlings who fetched him, grim-faced creatures with gelled hair and, expectedly, names of rock bands and European football clubs on their bursting T-shirts. To complete the common ensemble of Aparanta's enforcers and beachfront gigolos, they wear gold earrings, gold chains, cuffed denim jeans and square-toed boots. Sergei's two giant Russian guards are ranged behind the man, draped in leather. His girlfriend is absent.

The group is intimidating, but Dino is not Ida's son for nothing.

'Ah,' he says, with only a trace of a quaver, 'the high council of the Inquisition. Pleasure to meet you. What are you going to do, kill me?'

'Da,' Sergei is the first to respond, his voice slurred with drink. 'I think so. We will kill you.' He looks first at his two sidekicks before turning to Winston. 'Okay, no?'

Winston nods, speechless now that his quarry is in front of him.

'Where is Number One?' Dino is calm.

'*Who* dat?' Winston enquires, though he has a feeling he knows what Dino is talking about.

'Your good friend. And his cocksucker sidekick, the hardworking Vimochan-bab. How much will they finally make when you all are done? A billion rupees? Two? Must be goat-shit for you bastards.'

'You are a wise man.' Sergei says. He looks to Winston. 'Why waste time?'

'Why only?' agrees Winston. He grimaces, then, emboldened with the company, draws a forefinger across his throat. 'Bye-bye,

Mister Saving Man. Bluddy fool, id-*jut*.'

Dino tries to stand, and one of Winston's enforcers kicks him in the well of the knee. As Dino staggers, he is hit hard on the neck, making him fall in a heap on the floor. The enforcer replaces Dino's gag.

Winston steps in quickly, eager to establish control. '*I* tell to you hit? Mudder-fuck!' He backhands the enforcer, red-eyed, blinking hard. '*I* tell to you hit?'

'Sorry boss,' the enforcer apologizes.

'*I* tell to you when to hit, how to hit. You hit dis way, no?' Winston Almeida steps up to Dino and kicks him on his head. Then with footwork worthy of a player in Almeida U, he uses the toe of his two-toned patent leather shoe, the left, to raise Dino's head from the floor, and shoots a perfectly aimed gob of spit at his face. Winston walks away from Dino, back to his chair, and with a general wave, declares, 'Your turn, no?'

There is a frenzy. All but the enforcers and Winston gather around to kick Dino, some wordlessly, some calling him names in many tongues, mostly questioning his ancestry. The son of Ida can do nothing more than curl up as he once had in her womb, and think of death. They stop for a brief few moments, but not the Princess, who commands PI Fernandes to undress Dino, and as he lies there, pale, with bruises and blood marking his smooth-skinned body, the Princess removes her sarong in front of an astounded audience, gets on her knees and in one smooth motion spits on herself before forcing her way into Dino. Dino screams in pain. But the Princess continues, breasts heaving. PI Fernandes lowers himself to the floor to kiss the breasts. Even MB, eager for a handful he does not need to work for, reaches out for a fondle. The Princess shoos them all away. She pummels into Dino for a few minutes, in absolute silence except for her harsh intakes of breath and exhalation, muted agony from Dino and the soft swish of the antique fan, till she empties into him with a prolonged shout, her voice cracking. She then lies gently on his sweat-pearled back and places her head on Dino's after softly kissing his hair. Sergei begins to applaud, and after a few seconds the others tentatively join in, as the Princess gets up and walks with PI Fernandes to the adjacent bedroom to clean up. More drink is poured all around by the diminutive Anita, and for a short time Dino is forgotten.

But the interlude does not last long, as it is now Sergei's turn, as leader and grand inquisitor, to show what punishment is. It is for him a thing of grace and beauty. Making the floor bare of rugs and requesting a rubber sheet, which he correctly assumes the adventurous Princess will possess, he places Dino on his back over it, and takes out a slim knife with an ivory handle, its hilt glinting with the suggestion of gold. With theatrics that come naturally to him, Sergei turns it around for the blade to catch light, ensuring all eyes are drawn to the blade, sharp on both sides, with a deep notch on the tip. Then it is showtime.

'I now show you all how we teach in Russia,' Sergei announces. To Dino he says, 'You see too much, Mister Jesus Christ.'

With that, he firmly holds Dino's chin, and in two lazy movements, one straight and the second a reverse sweep, he uses the tip of the knife to scoop out Dino's eyes.

'You hear too much,' he says next.

As Dino vomits past his gag, and there is faeces now where the Princess once was, Sergei removes one ear, and then the other.

'You talk too much,' Sergei pronounces. As he removes Dino's gag, he sees that he does not need to do much, as the tongue is sliced through with pain, but just so his word is good, Sergei removes Dino's lips. By then the audience begins to leave the room, all except Sergei's thugs, Winston, the Princess and PI Fernandes. Such violence is beyond the comprehension of Winston's enforcers— usually practitioners of straightforward stabs to the sternum—and also of MB, for it is beyond the simple slashing of throat and tossing of grenade near schools and security posts he once practised and now merely encourages, as always, for the cause of freedom. As partners, it is a matter of honour for Winston and the Princess to stay, as departure would be taken as a sign of weakness—and who knows what terminal gifts might arrive from the Tsars. PI Fernandes stays because the hated Dino, cousin to the hated Tony Calangute, is down.

Sergei does much more, as a true teacher will, but by then his student is beyond lessons in art appreciation. Dino's life should flash in front of his eyes, as countless accounts claim, but as he escapes this existence Dino accepts that myth, too, to be a lie.

Much discussion follows Dino's passing.

'Take him away from here, you fool,' Sergei shouts, finished with his carving, washing the blood off his arms over the rubber sheet with French mineral water poured by his thug. 'Why did you not bring that girl? If she talks, I will talk to *you*, Mr Policeman. Where did you say you will take him?' He points to Dino.

'Chorao, no? Island it is.' PI Fernandes hastily offers.

'Then take him there and do something clever. I cannot understand why you let the girl go. She will talk. Do something. Is what we pay you for, no?'

'What dis?' PI Fernandes is hurt. 'You tink I am stupid? What you do wit no uniform?'

It is now the turn of Winston to lose his composure. He grabs PI Fernandes by the collar and lifts him up, dragging his shoes on the floor. 'If you *not* do someting, you lose dat uniform, and we get anudder uniform. Someone *not* stupid, no?'

He puts PI Fernandes down, grabs the gold chains the inspector wears and pulls viciously, tearing them off his neck and making him stagger into the Princess who holds onto him. She bites his left ear. Sergei guffaws at that, whisky glass in hand. But, strangely, Winston is sickened, and throws the chains in front of PI Fernandes before he walks off to the other end of the room.

'I take him,' PI Fernandes gets up, foaming, and rubs his neck. 'But for dis, you pay double. Dis not discount rate, okay? You tink I not keep record? You scratch my knee, I scratch your knee.'

'*Back*!' Winston screams. 'Back, id-*jut*! Go! Or I break your knee, no, mudder-fuck!'

Sergei is bent with laughter. He smashes his glass of whisky to the floor in mirth, and kicks the biggest shard into the wall with the toe of an alligator-skin boot. Iosif, who is standing by the wall where the glass strikes, jumps away to avoid the shard gouging his arm. He takes one look at the exuberant Sergei and decides it is better to keep his peace.

PI Fernandes releases himself from the Princess's embrace and glares at everyone before leaving. He escorts Dino, now neatly wrapped in the rubber sheet on which he visited the Lord, which is wrapped again in a colourful dhurrie for camouflage and to soak his blood, carried by Winston's enforcers. The demure Anita will soon be summoned to clear away the few spots Dino has left behind with a soak of strong detergent, cover any remaining signs with a carpet of glorious mandala and serve more drinks to all but MB, for he is a religious man.

'Go in peace, my love,' the Princess blows PI Fernandes a kiss. 'Adeus.'

25. PI Fernandes and Dionysus Take Some Water

And so it comes to pass that PI Fernandes and Dionysus Dantas journey together—PI Fernandes seated in front, next to an enforcer, who is driving Dino's Fiat, and Dino snugly curled in the trunk of his chariot, a place that he, with a quirk of postcolonial Britannia absorbed during his days in Bombay, called 'dicky'. The second enforcer is on the cramped back seat, while a third, Winston's personal chauffeur, follows in a black SUV.

It is not a pleasant ride for PI Fernandes, as the enforcers, partly fed by nervousness and partly by their imaginings of the inspector in dalliance with the Princess, occasionally joke about his ambivalent sexuality. PI Fernandes suffers in silence. It is a significant sacrifice because even at three in the morning the ride south from Mandrem to the ferry point for Chorao at Ribander, in the shadow of the ghosts of Goa Dourada, is a long and relatively slow one through winding village lanes. It will not do to have an accident with their cargo and an inspector, even one as variously protected as PI Fernandes. The cars pick up speed only when they join the north-south highway near the suburbs of Mapusa. It is quiet, and even the ageing chariot of Dino, as it precedes the noiseless SUV, is deferential to the heavy air. It absorbs sound, quickly erasing the passage of the cortege. The vehicles glide down the slope past Aparanta's assembly, playground of Number Ones and lesser (though no less squalid) numbers, and gently coast to a stop at a security checkpoint near the Mandovi Bridge. This surprises PI Fernandes, as he has been given to understand on good authority that there will be no checkpoints this night. So, as a policeman asks for the car's papers, the inspector is hysterical.

'You know who I am, no?' he screams. '*Who* am I?'

When his outburst fails to elicit a positive response, PI Fernandes, after years of policing, is compelled to proffer his proof of identity by pulling out a rarely used card—after all, who doesn't know PI Fernandes?—with his stern-faced photograph, and name in capital letters.

The enforcer on the driver's seat has his face turned away, PI Fernandes notices as they drive off, and he wonders at the strange itching he can feel at the back of his head. Was it a scratch from the long nails of the Princess from the previous evening, when (s)he had magnanimously permitted PI Fernandes to mount her in the missionary position so he could reach her boobies more easily? Or, was it the excess Ajinomoto in the Goan-Chinese takeaway meal the two had consumed after the missionary putting, courtesy of the talkative Tibetan chef at Chin Chin (Authentic Chinese Cuisine) in Mapusa? A nagging feeling that that might have been his last supper briefly crosses his mind.

The drive past the Ribander Circle is uneventful, and PI Fernandes finds the time to appreciate the beauty of lamppost-high cylinders of light Number One had ordered to be planted at the crossroads to celebrate the film festival at Aparanta. The pillars marked the passage to Bombay-then-Mumbai to the north, south through Salcette to land's end where the peninsula of India kisses the waves of Serendip, the way west to Dona Paula and the embrace of the ocean, and east to the Chorao ferry and further past the grand ruins of Dom Afonso's foray. The arrival at the ferry point of Chorao is equally devoid of drama. There is no one there, the ferries having ended work several hours earlier. 'All in all, it is working,' as Editor Rodrigues would typically conclude his laudatory editorials on government policy in *Goa Chronicle*. Certainly a fine night for Dino to go into his river of lament.

As the enforcer parks the car on the lip of the steep slope of the ferry landing, the SUV stops a few paces behind. Dino is removed from his rest and unfurled from the dhurrie in the shadow of the car, to be placed in the back seat of the Fiat. All this is done with minimum noise by two enforcers as the third continues to sit in the SUV. The car is then pushed, one enforcer turning the wheel from outside while the second pushes from behind, and the first quickly reaches past the wheel to pull up the handbrake as soon as the car is positioned for descent on the slope.

PI Fernandes misses this as he is engaged in urinating into a nearby hedge, and that is how he loses consciousness, penis in left hand, stream of urine momentarily distracted before resuming its flow in total detachment from the crushing blow to his head the third enforcer applies with a large hammer. So PI Fernandes unceremoniously visits the Lord, with urine on his hand, pants, shoes and the feet of some cranes on his prized shirt, a gift from the Princess. He is then placed behind the wheel. Windows are rolled down to ensure flooding. The handbrake is released to roll forward Dionysus's chariot, driven by the Princess's consort now firmly in the logbooks of the protectors of Aparanta, his face registering mild surprise at being interrupted at susu.

With the daintiest of splashes, PI Fernandes, along with Dionysus, smoothly disappears into the Mandovi.

26. Carmelito and Caxinata are Acquainted with D. Dantas

'Nature takes care of one's own,' the Professor solemnly announced later that day at Happy Bar, where friends and lovers of Dino, including Charming and Tilly, participated in a wake so profound it was feared all Aparanta would run dry of emotion and alcohol.

But before we return to the Professor, Dino's discovery needs a mention.

Taken by the tide from his beloved Fiat and from PI Fernandes—the policeman still pinned by the steering wheel to the bottom of the Mandovi—Dino has drifted downstream and snagged on the debris of old construction, there from the time the Mandovi Bridge fell down when he was still a young man in Bombay. One span had grown to two, but the jumble of concrete remained, and rusted iron and steel that fishing trawlers, barges and pleasure craft take care to avoid. But Dino has found these, and is thus discovered instead of being flushed out of the Mandovi into the lesser cesspool of the sea.

As its happens, Carmelito Sequeira and Caxinata Cuncoliencar, old friends and neighbours at the charming, crumbling ward of São Tomé (a picture of relative communal amity to the general consternation of those like Number One on the one hand and evangelical Christendom on the other), are out line-fishing along the eastern span of the Mandovi Bridge. They are present here every day at dawn, even on days dawn is abolished by rain that blinds the keenest crow and barge-master.

Caxinata sees Dino first, drawn by the cackle of the usually quiet cormorant and kingfisher that wait on stilts by the banks along the road from Panjim to Ribander. Looking down, he sees dozens of birds respectfully crowding a body dressed in white shirt and dark pants—it is still too dark to make out the colours beyond the basic—as it lies half out of the water. Caxinata calls out to Carmelito. Their fishing is soon forgotten, as is their fishing tackle and the thermos of strong black coffee they took turns to brew on alternate days to spare their wives grief of an earlier than usual awakening. They run the rolling run of elderly men to the police checkpoint at the Panjim end of the bridge. Finding nobody there, the two friends, hearts and minds racing with enhanced power, carry on towards the nearby exit to Ribander, knowing a policeman or two may be lurking there to pluck early morning traffic violators. They find none.

That drives the two further afield, by now their hearts pumping blood at pressure unfamiliar for many years. They head as fast as they can towards the Old Secretariat, which stands on the ruins of the palace of Dom Afonso's Idalcão, the hapless Ismail Adil Shah of the kingdom of Bijapur and ejected overlord of Aparanta. Finally, they spot a police jeep, where the two pour out information in a rapid-fire mix of Konknni, Portuguese and English and are soon witness to a wondrous sight: policemen of Aparanta roaring into action, the superior officer pulling on the handset of a dashboard-recessed communicator to immediately report the matter to headquarters and urging Carmelito and Caxinata to get in the back of the jeep. With a dramatic screech of tyres, they make for the jetty near the office of the captain of ports.

Carmelito and Caxinata would have many stories to tell their families later that day, and for many days afterwards. Accorded VIP status by the police, they were brought to a small launch and on that they travelled upriver towards the mess of fallen bridge-support that held the body. When they arrived a few minutes later, they saw that a large crowd had gathered on the bridge and briefly wondered about their tackle and thermos.

As the boat approached the body, the helmsman got a little nervous, earning a stern query from the captain of the boat, Bernardo Bhobo, normally a grizzled terror of the quayside and occasional drinking mate of Carmelito and Caxinata at the Santa Rita, as to whether he was driving his youngest aunty's bum. It was a sight worthy of nerves. After all, how many people have feasted their eyes on a corpse watched over by great numbers of kingfisher and cormorant—nature's unabashed sun-worshippers—now just content to hold their wings wide to shield the body in the fading dark? They could see the shirt now, more muddy than white. It was torn, stained red as if with spat-out betel juice that colours the walls and sidewalks of the subcontinent. The jeans were impeccable even after the trauma of death, but the feet and hands were horrors. The face, drowned-white like the feet and hands, was so evocative it set Carmelito to repeatedly mutter 'Mãe de deus', Caxinata to deposit remnants of his dinner of peerless chicken xacuti from Anandashram into the burdened Mandovi, and Captain Bhobo to exclaim, 'By my great aunty's bum, God in heaven!' to nobody in particular.

The noisy birds at vigil finally let the body go when two helpers dragged it feet first off the rubbish pile of concrete and metal, limp, like it did not any more have a bone. The police found a wallet in the back pocket of the jeans, containing a little less than three hundred rupees, an ATM card and a driving licence with a face that looked quite removed from the horrors, and a name: D. Dantas.

When the police boat turned around, deftly manoeuvring in the wash of a procession of barges returning empty from their transfer to giant ships bound for China and Japan out in harbour and open sea, a few dozen of the birds glided in to take position on various perches on the boat. They remained until D. Dantas was taken on a stretcher into an ambulance. Even after that, Carmelito and Caxinata would later swear to friends and family, some lingered, as if unsure where to go, homeless, lost.

27. When Does Ida's Hair Turn White Only?

D. Dantas is claimed a little after noon by G. Dantas, F/o, as the grief-mute advocate writes in the police form after he identifies his son's body at the morgue of Goa Medical College.

It had taken some hours even for the well-connected Gabru to trace Dino. Anjali had been up by six, playing with flowers in the porch and had rushed teary-eyed towards Tilly-mummy when she saw her, to say Dino-daddy still hadn't come home. Tilly had taken Anjali in her arms, marched into the house and demanded of Gabru, who by force of habit was seated with a cup of coffee and *Goa Chronicle,* to trace his missing son, because her tales of distress from the previous night were real. Then she locked eyes with Ida, who shrugged to signal to her that Gabru was in denial and drew Tilly and Anjali into the house. Anastasia was already there, and they were soon joined by Tony, who had reluctantly left the Villa in the Professor's care.

Driven by the urging of the ladies, Gabru and Tony telephoned again the high and relatively low—police, lawyers and officials—at the police stations at Sodomo, Calangute, Mapusa and Panjim, but without success. They then retired to the comfort of the master bedroom. Tony the entertainer updated everyone on the antics of the Professor, and Melba, who seemed daily to be losing weight, Tony explained after covering Anjali's ears, with the 'sleepy-fuck' virus, triggering an uncharacteristic gale of laughter from the taciturn Gabru.

The call came at eleven in the morning, from Gabru's lawyer

friend Alito Cordeiro. 'Ay Gabru. I am so sorry amigo, they have found Dino,' Advogado Cordeiro was polite, soothing. 'It is some kind of terrible accident. I am so sorry…if there is anything I can do, he is, was—is, no?—mãe de deus, what is happening to us, he was, he *is,* like my son…'

Gabru had thanked him in a strong voice and, without saying another word or looking anyone in the eye, replaced the phone in its cradle and marched off through the balcão and down the stairs to get his yellow Volkswagen Beetle from the garage. Ida and Tilly insisted on coming along, and Tony as well in his jeep. They left a hysterical Anjali in the care of Anastasia and drove to the Medical College, Ida riding silently with Gabru, a gentle hand on his shoulder, and Tilly with Tony, thoughts of Dino burning her, wetting her eyes because the tears would not be stayed any more—the calming presence of the innkeeper was too much impetus. She shook till she felt she would come unhinged and collapse in a heap on the floorboard of the jeep, while the innkeeper drove with death in his heart.

Gabru was the first to come upon the eyeless Dionysus, for only one person per cadaver is allowed inside the morgue at one time. And then, in turn, came Ida, Tilly and Tony. By the time D. Dantas was wheeled out on a gurney, a hearse awaited him, arranged by Advogado Cordeiro who had thoughtfully rung for Lobo's Hearse Service, a dedicated manager of His travel agency.

Ida grieved silently over her son's body, gently closing his eyes, with a little difficulty as the lids were ragged and limp from lost support, then running her fingers delicately over a face scarred numerously with cuts and puffy with water. She buttoned what remained of his shirt to cover what remained of his torso, inflicted with similar cuts. Her face didn't change in expression. She silently rested her head on her son's chest and took him in her arms as a sobbing Tilly held her. Tony, mind blank with rage, fought the urge to vomit and jammed his fists into the pockets of his Bermuda shorts so he would not strangle the first person he saw and held culpable for the death of Aparanta.

And, this day, Schubert Lobo was able to offer a rare 'companion free' passage, only the third since establishing his partnership firm for funerary services in the fading days of empire. For, seeing the hurt and grief on the face of his wife, his son's lover, and cousin and best friend, Gabru Dantas quietly went to the Lord. He did so like a gentleman, not making a fuss. When he decided it was past injury-time, he staggered to the nearest wall and, as others stood looking at the reduced Dino, Gabru slid down to the floor.

In a few minutes Ida came upon her husband, as did others, drawn by the commotion immediately to their right as onlookers discovered Gabriel. As always, his elegant straw hat was upright, his eyes peacefully open, a little dab of blood at one nostril the only sign of a squall in his patrician head, dislodging a few Mangalore roof tiles, cracking a beam or two, an ancient house weakened with callous and continuous roadworks near its foundation, his time done. Ida removed the hat and gently wiped the blood off Gabru's face, and kneeling there she held his hands in hers.

Some hospital orderlies would swear Ida Dantas's hair went white in front of their eyes. But it could have been the play of the fierce noonday sun. Ida looked almost relieved, the orderlies maintained, that she would not have to grieve twice over.

◆

Later that day, others would claim Ida's hair turned white as she saw the bodies of her son and husband burn in the Hindu crematorium of Sodomo. The change of colour would show through the fine black veil that covered her head—but that could have been a sleight of light and lace, as it was towards the end of the day.

Not wishing the flesh and bones of her husband and son to be placed near the bones of Number Ones (which would be inevitable in Saligao as a former Number One lived there), as that would be heaping indignity on insult, Ida took the decision, instead, to cremate them. When Father Gonsalves tried to intervene, saying it would be proper for the sons of Saligao to be buried in the pretty cemetery across the road from the pretty church—was it not the best-maintained church in all Goa?—Ida, losing composure for the first of two times that day, screamed, 'Ele é um merdas, no?'

The former Number One followed, trying to calm her down, but by force of habit it came out as an admonishment, a command further reinforced by the wagging of a directorial forefinger, and Ida screamed at him as well, insisting, 'a prostitute has greater honour'. Nobody disagreed with the assessment, though her address to Father Gonsalves in Portuguese, calling him a real shit, needed translation for many who had gathered and brought spontaneous applause for the emphatic Ida. Tony then suggested cremating Gabriel and Dino in Sodomo, after, of course, asking Perpet Saibinn's permission. Escorted by him, Ida visited the Saibinn's place, with Tilly, Bing and Ujjwala adding to the small team—a sedated Anjali by then taken away by Anastasia to her parents, the gracious Benedito and Inacia, at Raia.

But Father Gonsalves, slow to learn and eager to protect his charge, was already at the Saibinn's, and, along with Janardan Naik, tried to block their way a good distance from the place of worship.

'*How* you can do?' Naik demanded, outraged by this blurring of religious lines he worked hard to preserve and annoyed that Tony would presume to blur these lines without even a hint of grease. 'You aks my permissions, boss?'

'*How* you can, bluddy hell?' Father Gonsalves stood by Janardan Naik, unmindful of blasphemy. 'No aks, just do-do-do?'

It was an intemperate thing to say, for Tony Calangute, at six feet four inches and weighing in at nearly one hundred kilograms, plucked Father Gonsalves off the ground with one hand and flung him to the ground. The crowd, by then numbering nearly a hundred, roared in approval of Tony, and some laughed, seeing glimpses of the bright-red innerwear of Father Gonsalves. Janardan Naik fled towards the Saibinn, followed by Tony and a cheering crowd. Tony soon caught up with him, and did not require further prompting to walk into Janardan Naik, leaving him unconscious and bleeding by the side of the Saibinn's door, an arm, jaw and, as it would turn out, the lower right portion of his ribcage, needing repair.

Tony then escorted Ida and Tilly to meet the Saibinn.

Perhaps Ida Dantas's hair changed to white as she sat across from the Saibinn and talked to her, one mother to another, about the infinity of love and justice. But it is difficult to be certain of such things, especially in the dancing, misleading light of candles.

28. All Souls' Day at Happy Bar

The day is extraordinary, and so Villa de Vida is thrown open to all. Even those who run the folk music school behind Boom Shack that sometimes robs the peace of mind of guests at the Villa with monotonous trance-induced beating of all manner of drums.

Marietta, belly dancer from the old city of Cologne, holds court, like a mourning swan in flowing black skirt. She does not mind when a guest at the Villa, Jean-Pierre Gardaz, a doctor of hearts from the northern shores of Lake Geneva, rests his head, unasked, on her bosom. Youngman Mark is present with Eremita from Santiago, Chile, Sally having returned to England after an overdose of karma and carrot cake absorbed in the Himalayan foothills. Readmitted to the Villa, Mark has ordered for the wake a bottle of Happy Bar's best cashew feni and is well travelled through it. Florian and his devoted partner, Rainer, take solace in the finest marijuana from Kerala, otherwise taboo at Happy Bar. In short, the passing of Dionysus Dantas has changed many equations, and Happy Bar is part of that universal matrix.

Antonio has initiated the celebration. His nose, hair and lungs still consumed with the smell of the burning Dionysus and Gabriel, the innkeeper had journeyed to talk to the Dom, a distraught Zezito refusing to go any further beyond the first line of coconut palms, after promising Anastasia that he would not allow patrao to walk into the sea. He had assured her, when, frantic with concern, she had telephoned the Villa from Raia, as Tony would not answer his cell phone. Anjali, still sunk in Dino-sleep, was in her arms and she was too laden with grief to cope with another final solution that day.

The Dom had arrived quickly, facilitated by superior feni, and not wasted any time with preliminaries.

'Dis Dino, no? What they did to him?' he had asked gruffly. '*How* he will see dere wit no eyes and all, bugger? And what about his daddy? He has special requests or what? We have request cards for new people up there, VIP on first day.' Then he decided to be solicitous to the living. 'Antonio, my son. Ay, Antonio? You listening, or you dying-dying also and coming home to the Lord, leaving dat beautiful wife—Dona Anastasia.'

'You must have made the men on your ships go insane with talk.'

'Control the fluttering of your tongue or I will find a new species of shark to feed it to, and perhaps your pirilau too.' The Dom, suddenly formal, sat directly in front of Tony on a Vietnamese woven cane chair from the day room at the Villa, billowing a fuller beard than Tony had seen before. He inhaled deeply and puffed out his chest. 'You know not how many I have killed to secure the Estado da India, or my pride. How does it matter if I kill one more blackie?'

'I'm brown, can't you see?'

'That is because a drop or two of my blood is in yours, and that is enough to secure your future. Have you applied yet for a Portuguese passport, silly boy?' The Dom slips once again into patois. 'I will endorse it also and you will get it fast-fast.'

'Take it easy.'

'*What* easy, men? You peoples worried about black Christian, brown Christian, dis-dat. For us, no, all you peoples black, Cristão preto. Colony is colony, no? Indu peoples and Moorish peoples becoming Cristão, my Jesu being happy boy, my Catarina smiling also. So all dis brown-black, *what* matters?'

Laughter was forced from Tony. 'You win.' Then he noticed

the Dom's face. 'You grew your beard some more or what, chief?'

'What to do, boss?' the Dom had exhaled with a long, low whistle. 'Some peoples etching and painting and carving me dis way, some dat.' He loudly breathed in and out again. 'I can't get angry like old times, no? All dis drama I can't do. Maybe I try some yoga, some pranayama, like your friend—what her name? Michelle, she teaches here in the morning. What she wears, my son, one-piece top and one-piece bottom, her boobies making nice holiday. We have carnaval, and I be King Momo and dis Michelle be Queen Momee, no, ha-ha. What dat ting?'

'Bikini,' Tony said. 'Nice, no?'

'Si, nice. You like? Dona Anastasia not minding?'

'She can't see, no? Onions and all.'

'Too much,' the Dom agreed. 'But now she has a daughter again, so she will soon be whole again. Then both of you can do fing-fing only for fun, no need to make babies, bugger what dese big hat peoples are saying.'

Tony had laughed at the thought of the Dom taking issue with Oldman Benedict. The woodcut smiled, very pleased with his joke. They had settled into companionable silence, the sort Tony would sometimes enjoy with Francesco. But the Dom, always eager to be heard, had refused to be silent for long.

'Dionysus made you whole in death, no?'

Tony had choked with anger. 'Dino and Uncle Gabru are both dead. Have you fucking *seen* Dino? They cut off half his body. You call this whole, you idiot-bastard?'

'If I did not love you like my own son, I would have you hanged, quartered, and then flushed you down the Idalcão's potty for insulting me.'

'You're not helping.'

'But what I tell you, no, dis Dino has made y'all whole,' the Dom had switched back to informal. 'He die, daddy die and now all Goa getting *so-lid* mad.'

'What do you mean?'

'Look at you, bashing peoples. *When* last time you hit someone? Dat tief who took coconuts from Casa Serena, and Deodato Pinto in school, no, for putting scorpion in your bum-pocket?'

'We're going to do a party for Dino at Happy Bar. What you think?'

'I think it's a glorious idea. Man must be mourned with drink and cheer because God does bugger-all, I tell you,' the Dom concluded. 'You see what will happen, my son. Dionysus will create history, and I can tell you, my angry pup, I know quite a lot about that.'

The Dom is right.

They start to arrive a little after Marietta begins to dance, first to the rhythm of the djembe, and then to rhythmic claps at Happy Bar, word of the wake having taken wing on the mystery-winds of Aparanta. Many come with candles, Tony sees, slim sticks, fattened wax, even elegant aromatherapy circles that otherwise float in evenings in the resorts and genteel homes. Those who have more share with those who have none.

Slowly, a sea of firefly-fire spreads beyond Tony's line of sight, from areas of dark to light, moving further from Happy Bar in a tide. Gradually, it captures all of Sodomo, then reaches through serpent lanes to Arpora, north up the hill of Parra, then the land from Assagao to Mapusa, and to Anjuna, where birds in droves desert the revelry at the midweek flea market. And still more come towards Happy Bar, as restaurants, hotels and homes of Bardez begin to empty, and many in Salcette and other talukas too.

It is a great tide of light. It is difficult to point out its origin, but it is soon everywhere and then the source no longer matters as it washes towards and away from Happy Bar with such force that Tony is moved to tears. He stands hugging Anastasia, Tilly and the widow Charming as they too weep for a son of Aparanta.

When the candles dim many hours later, the light remains, seared into memory. And later still, when the full Cheddar-yellow moon is overhead and Marietta is sunk into her pool of dancer's black, when birds return to their nests, the empty lanes of Aparanta are still full of vision.

29. Aparanta Pokes Some People in the Bum

It is not known what causes it, but history is shaped in the days After Dionysus, to be marvelled at by recorders and claimed as divination by necromancers.

The Professor has an explanation for the developments. 'It is like the rain,' he tells visitors at Happy Bar. 'Eight months of dirt and derision is washed away in a few days. But this isn't water doing the cleansing any longer, my friends. It is the land, angry to bloody-fuck hell, no?'

By common consent of the management of the Villa, comprising Antonio de Calangute and the benign presence of Afonso de Albuquerque, the Professor is these days restricted to late hours, when patrons are more likely to welcome gutter-speak from the soul. But whatever the Professor's eloquence, it is said more simply by others: That it is all caused by Aparanta 'with a little help from the spirits of Gabru and Dino poking bad people in the bum and all'.

◆

The turning to ash of Dino and Gabru is marked annually with a peculiar procession of the devout, women above the age of eighteen, from all faiths. They first collect near the panchayat office of Sodomo, then visit Perpet Saibinn to ask her blessings, depositing lit candles at her feet. They then move to the small temple to Manguesh only a turn away from the crematorium, with offerings of fresh poyee and red hibiscus. They carry on to the end of the winding road, past Stanley's Homely and Timely Store, past

Villa de Vida, past Boom Shack, rhythmically clapping their hands and singing a lilting song from the eastern hills of Aparanta that speaks of a man's love for his land and how the land claimed him when his duty was done. At the headland, the women sing some more as they face the ocean.

But all do not stand so peacefully. The grand tradition of the Sodomo zatra evolves, with between two and three dozen women (which over time grows to hundreds) burning three straw effigies placed on stakes at the headland, accompanied by much cursing, pounding of chest and tearing of hair. On one effigy is written the word 'Winston', the second has written on it 'Police/Drug'—folklorists have yet to resolve if it means law enforcement is like a drug or that they go hand in hand—while the third effigy has 'Number One' in cross-hatched American fashion for 'number' followed by the numeral. After half an hour or so the ritual ends with the sprinkling of seawater over the remains of the effigies, and the resolute women disperse into the paddies and by-lanes to take Aparanta's well-being into their own hands.

Rapidly, the ritual finds its way into guidebooks. Unlucky tourists who have missed the November event clutch updated editions of *Lonely Planet*, *The Rough Guide*, *Le Guide du Routard* and numerous other guidebooks in major languages of the world and retrace the walk, laden with tiny backpacks. And Sodomo, which enters lore in this morph, is transformed from sleepy backwater to stylish destination that abounds in incredible stories and an arresting breed of storytellers at various bars who claim to be directly anointed by the legendary Professor.

◆

By popular consent, Ida Dantas is appointed the new chairperson of the Save Goa Society. It has been rid of its cabal of Winston-converts by a group of outraged readers of *Goa Chronicle* who turn livid after the publication of a three-part article by Ida initially titled 'The Song of Dionysus' but changed by a crafty newsdesk to a banner headline. 'How My Son and Husband were Killed as Goa Watched: A Mom's True Story'. The furious group storms a meeting of the society and ejects the trustees. This happens just days before a public interest litigation at court prevents these worthies from ever receiving funds from state agencies or overseas donors.

Ida is aided at Save Goa Society by its new secretary, Shakuntala Singh, now Tilly-mummy to Anjali and resident with Ida, the little girl a trifle recovered as the adopted daughter of Nasty-mummy and Tony Calangute. Miraculously, every adventure of the sisterhood of Ida and Tilly to cleanse Aparanta turns out successful, drawing people from the cities and villages, old and young, to rid the land of waste, detritus of mining, prevent conversion of a majority of agricultural and forest land for construction despite the best efforts of Franklin and his patron, the minister for town and country planning and New Number One.

Ida and Tilly also pressure New Number One and the Assembly of Aparanta to enforce stricter laws against the abuse of women and children and this, along with their collective action, brings for Ida, in rapid succession, the Ramon Magsaysay Award, the Sydney Peace Prize and an award from the Rockefeller Foundation. Yet, even today, the people of Aparanta point to a deal between snow-haired Ida and the wax-covered Saibinn, that public anger now has sanction of the Son of God—the Saibinn's baby with the crown of thorns. But in the manner of legends this conspiracy is never proved.

◆

The innkeeper, Tony Calangute, is now a legend in these parts. He features in guidebooks, and is held up as a role model for modern-day bikers of Aparanta. His legend is further enhanced when he embarks to fulfil the prophecy of PI Fernandes.

After a night of intense lovemaking with the surprised and delighted Anastasia, with the arrival of the rays of Sol and two kingfishers on the balcão, like heralds of good fishing, Tony begins scripting a tiatr that would soon be fêted as a modern classic. *Bhaxonn*, or *The Speech*, on the politics and pleasures of Aparanta, would open to full houses wherever it travelled. Critics would write of its passionate songs, its biting soliloquies on Aparanta's condition, its open and merciless detraction of Number Ones, the various evils of a man called Churchill Almeida (the name masked to prevent accusations of libel by the family of Winston), and the tragic life and death of Dionysus to reclaim the pride of Aparanta from these vermins.

Tony's creative pursuit is helped immensely by the radical change in atmosphere at the Casa Serena, his divided home, brought forth by the voting out of Janardan Naik as sarpanch of Sodomo. Lost without her anchor, and deserted by her goats who suddenly display a marked lack of enthusiasm for Oedipal behaviour, Melba voluntarily withdraws to her former modest home. From there she desultorily runs her restaurant until one day, fulfilling Antonio's curse (this too added to his legend), she dies of pneumonia encouraged by the sleepy-fuck virus.

◆

A prospective Number One having taken away majority in the assembly of Aparanta with the help of all former Number Ones barring the first, who was long ago called away by the Lord—and the second, to whom no one any longer paid attention—our Recent Number One departs from his palace at Altinho even before it is time for migratory birds to return the following season.

Surprisingly, New Number One declines to enter into an understanding with Recent Number One, mentor to Vimochan

Sardessai and associate of Winston Almeida. New Number One grandly declares that Aparanta will henceforth be free of plastic bags, swine will not be used as collectors of refuse, and the children of Aparanta will as best as possible be shielded from procurers and molesters and the licences of partnering shack owners and innkeepers immediately cancelled if they are caught pandering to paedophiles, whether foreign or home-grown. They might even be jailed with the 'sickos', to use a term dear to Dionysus. New Number One also bans by decree all construction in the name of development and tourism without scrutiny by referees of the public. As these measures will change the face of Aparanta and return it in great part to being Goa Dourada, the people rejoice. Those who know the manner of Number Ones look for signs of accommodation, but agree it will only be polite to wait for a few weeks to pass such judgement and call New Number One a thief and liar.

Meanwhile, dispossessed of his throne and livid with RCs for stabbing him in the back, Recent Number One sets about the destruction of all street names in Portuguese or otherwise glorifying the children of Dom Afonso in Panjim's Fontainhas, a charming ward of narrow lanes coloured by houses of blue, yellow, ochre, brick-red and white. He is photographed by alert teams from *Goa Chronicle* personally breaking tiles bearing colonial street names and the window panes at the residence of the deputy consul of Portugal. His glory lasts only a few short days, however, as *Goa Chronicle* quickly erupts in a frenzy of newsbreaks, unprecedented in its relatively short, inaccurate and cowed life, discovered courtesy of rousing back-channel diplomacy between Editor Rodrigues and emissaries of New Number One. This takes place at the elegant Horse Shoe Restaurant on Rua de Ourem, not too far from where the eyeless Dionysus was discovered. The news: Recent Number One's son-in-law has accepted citizenship of Portugal, keen to leverage the ever-expanding European Union. Stung, Recent Number One issues a full-page advertisement of remorse in the daily which is always glad to paper over blinding ironies in the interest of fair play and advertising revenue. Following this, Recent Number One resigns state leadership and primary membership of his party. He is last heard of as having taken residence with a yoga guru in the holy city of Rishikesh, but the knowledgeable few are aware of other spiritual journeys: occasional forays to Dubai for a little putting and meetings with personal bankers. At any rate, he is never again seen in Aparanta.

◆

Recent Number One's associate, Vimochan Sardessai, mysteriously takes ill from the effects of the sleepy-fuck virus. As he wastes away discreetly in a hospital at Belgaum in the neigbouring state of Karnataka, his family puts out word that Sardessai has departed for an extended sabbatical to the United States of America to visit his youngest daughter, a well-settled anaesthetist. However, all covers are blown by an enterprising reporter of the newly robust *Goa Chronicle* which obtains hospital records and even a photograph of the man in his plastic tent, delicately sneezing his life away.

◆

Winston Almeida retreats to Salcette in the company of his new mistress, Lily, being told by messengers of New Number One, duly pressured by worthies at the GGCCII, that if he were to take a step north of the Zuari River for reasons of business, the state would not take responsibility for what happened to him. Winston has become a liability, linked to all manner of unsavoury practices that *Goa Chronicle* excavates with blazing regularity—driving Editor Rodrigues to drink more on account of increased work and inability to deal with fame. But these worthies have been in turn pressured by the storm called Dionysus, in the form of a long-mouldering petition in the Aparanta bench of the Bombay High Court that speaks of a conspiracy to lay waste Aparanta by the sea and of the involvement of Winston, high ministers, lawkeepers and sundry trustees of Save Goa Society. Another petition speaks of the need to adopt environment-friendly practices at their mining operations and stop indentured labour, or face closure.

(This, among other things, causes such consternation that a distracted Zuarinagarcar misses his footing while alighting from his yacht at Aguada and breaks his ankle. And MJ, after an unsatisfying meal of caldeirada one early evening, bites too hard on his houseboy's penis, leading the young man in deep pain to clap his hands on MJ's head, causing him deafness.)

But Winston's ambition will not let him fester in tiny Salcette after the near-conquest of north Goa. Desperate for expansion, he cuts into the territory of the slumlord-garbage contractor from Margao, from whom he had earlier grabbed the gold-coloured car. He sees this move as an opportunity to again break into the lowermost strata of Aparanta, always good political fodder, for he has by now tired of the weaknesses of Number Ones and harbours thoughts of one day emerging as Number One himself. With the power of the slums and migrant labour that services the garbage operation, he believes, he just might be able to pull it off. Sharing his plain thinking with Iosif and Franklin, he says, 'Why be Number Two, Tree, Four, Fie only, when you can be Number One, no?'

The slumlord, however, gets wind of Winston's ambition and, in a gambit that would have made Winston's guru proud, invites Winston to his lair for a summit sans advisers. Whereupon Winston, in a gesture of unbridled idiocy, drives over grandly with only one thug as protection, waving at crowds who he thinks will once again be his by the end of the day. However, after the leader and his thug are escorted into the slumlord's office near the landfill, they are quickly bludgeoned to unconsciousness and spirited away through the backdoor to be buried, mouth and limbs trussed with stout rope, under a mound of fresh refuse of Aparanta which will never be recycled. So, Winston and his thug go to maggots without discovery. Their mobile phones are crushed and Winston's SUV driven away to the southern jungles and dumped by a Winston look-alike who wears surgical gloves to prevent disturbing any Almeida Bros fingerprints. It is as if Winston has never existed. The slumlord maintains to an agitated Iosif, Franklin and their thugs that Winston and his guard had departed, at Winston's express wish, after an unconsummated deal—and there is little the brothers can do except scream obscenities. When the SUV is finally discovered several days later by the police, it is confiscated as evidence, and word mysteriously travels to Iosif and Franklin not to probe the issue or instigate a war. Just shut up and let go, to live.

◆

With the dramatic non-existence of Winston, Iosif retires to a life of supervising petty extortion in Varca, where he takes to riding about in open-topped jeeps wearing wrap-around sunshades, sporting a titch of triangular goatee and changing his bandana each day. He also attempts to manage the fortunes of Almeida U, which has lost its fine touch and is continuously threatened with relegation at national football tournaments. Iosif's public outbursts at referees—a practice absorbed from Winston—have no effect. For some mysterious reason the referees refuse any longer to be threatened or bribed by an Almeida, and the once-adoring public wonder what their club has done wrong to deserve this fate.

Some point to articles in *Goa Chronicle* that allude to threats and blackmail being key ingredients to the success of Almeida U, others to editorials that speculate about Winston coming to a sticky end or being on the run to escape an Interpol alert. But purists write that off to the jealousy of rivals. At any rate few will any more turn to look when Iosif goes past in his jeep and that will upset him so much he will neglect to cover his shaved pate with a bandana, further adding to anonymity. There are now so many like him, just another thug in the anus of Aparanta.

Surprisingly, Franklin, of lower key among the Almeida brothers, proves to be more industrious than Iosif, using forgery and legal recourse to eject a family from their mansion at Taleigao, just downwind from Panjim, and begin rule as public benefactor in that patch of north Goa. His victims speak of him in hushed tones and give him whatever land he asks for, preferring to sell and migrate elsewhere in Aparanta and the beckoning cities of India and the world than to deal with coercion, broken limbs and sudden death. In that, little has changed from one Almeida to another. But Franklin is clever. He keeps the coercion discreet, shares fragrant grease more generously and takes recourse to ensuring perfect paperwork by any means. He can be seen riding one of his three SUVs, seated at the back with darkened window rolled down, waving regally at his subjects with his right hand while he strokes a new affectation, a pencil-thin moustache, with his left.

Bereft of true leadership in the form of the once-legendary Winston and spineless Number Ones, Franklin's delicate yet emphatic moustache and ready smile offer his admirers hope. They speak of him as adviser to Number One and, more significantly, confidante of the new minister of town and country planning, always a prime post for the rape of Aparanta and perpetuation of the great principle of more power to the powerful. After all, this is a man Number Ones, past, present and aspirational, come to for advice. He builds parks, schools and auditoria. Who else has done so much in such a short time?

Meanwhile, Lumena, the long-suffering wife of the disappeared Winston, and her brood, Tojo, Tito and Tarzan, emerge as impressive landlords in Salcette. For Winston, in an attempt to mask ownership and source of funds, has developed most properties in the name of his immediate family. Naturally, these now come to them, and Lumena, in a gesture that makes her the star of the parish and her children the toast of Sunday school, offers Lily, Winston's mistress, continued residence at the same apartment where Winston had housed her. Lumena is promptly featured on the cover of the Sunday edition of *Goa Chronicle,* along with her views on everything from what she does on Sundays—'I spend time with my Gods, childrens and also go to Fifi's to manicure-pedicure only'—to her favourite label, Dolce & Gabbana, bought from the pavement during visits to Bangkok.

◆

A week after the death of Dionysus, Sergei Yurlov, the viceroy of trance, is discovered in the laundry room of the Hotel Ukraina in Moscow. His associate, the divine Victoria of the boobie-bells, is pulled out by a boathook the same morning from the Moskva River. Both sport a bullet hole each in their throats, a farewell gift after a hurried departure from Aparanta. Suitably briefed, newspapers (*Goa Chronicle* among these) urinate on truth by classifying the deaths as street revenge for a high-class prastitutka and her overreaching svodnik.

Word arrives gradually to Aparanta: Sergei's overlords were displeased at his indiscretions and overt habits. The new viceroy in Aparanta by the sea would need to possess greater powers of control. In accordance, the charter company owned by Sergei is deliberately bankrupted and made to be reborn to provide the new viceroy with freshly laundered clothes and funds. There is implied promise through roundabout sources of Sergei's debts coming good if relationships develop and enrichment for the new viceroy and his overlords is assured.

The Princess, though ever eager for new allies, withdraws from the public eye after the departure of PI Fernandes and Dionysus—followed rapidly by that of Sergei and his mistress. She forsakes even her Sunday ritual of breakfast at Lila Cafe overlooking Sodomo Creek, at a small table at the back, away from curious eyes. After a desultory few weeks of mildly rekindled love with her maid Anita, the Princess is found dead in her purple Land Rover at the bottom of Bambolim Plateau, where the curving road from Goa Medical College begins to kiss the quiet village of Siridao.

There are no marks of injury, which on the face of it rules out death caused by jealous lovers or business partners—even the police—but one never knows these days, with natural and manmade poisons about. There is also talk that the Princess died of sheer boredom, but to many that is too simplistic an explanation. At any rate, a post-mortem is ordered to hush findings, and before being packed off to a crematorium at government expense the unclaimed body of the Princess provides the last few raised eyebrows at the autopsy table at Goa Medical College, where comments range from '*How* can…' to 'Oof', gossip duly published in *Goa Chronicle.*

And so we come to the new queen of trance in Goa, Anita. Even without her mistress's remarkable appendage she displays supreme wisdom. When police swoop on Avenida Srinagar, picking up MB and three of his colleagues (they simply disappear) and threaten other colleagues with closure and disappearance if they peddle anything other than products of carved wood and lambswool, the queen-on-the-make does not lift a finger in their support. There will always be more couriers in Avenida Srinagar, she reasons to the new viceroy of the Tsars, there will always be policemen to bend. This is just a public show of umbrage by New Number One.

Give it time, she tells him. In the dispensable, circular nature of things, there is always time.

30. The End

One evening, Tony Calangute, his bride Anastasia, and their daughter Anjali, walk the clean sands of Socorro Do Mundo holding hands in the contented nature of things, the Dom invites himself with a gentle knock as the family passes Dominic's orange fishing boat. Antonio misses a step in surprise, which brings a look of concern to Anastasia's face and stops Anjali in the act of picking up a still damp starfish from its subtle indentation in the sand.

'Ay, Dom, long time, boss,' our Tony greets him, his eyes briefly glazing before he catches himself and stays rooted. 'What happened?'

'Nutting baba, what is dere?' the Dom says, with an indulgent glance at Anastasia and Anjali. He casually inspects his fingernails and looks out to sea, this day a little driven with breeze. 'I'm dere, no?'

Acknowledgements

This is a story worth retelling.

The Baptism of Tony Calangute was in an earlier avatar *Once Upon a Time in Aparanta*, a title I disliked, but my publisher at the time appeared to think it suitably mysterious. At any rate it proved to be misplaced faith, as the book journeyed from its first home with what I took to be shabby understanding and care in reaching it to readers. It drove me in desperation to withdraw the book from circulation, despite the dedicated following and appreciation it had gathered. My apologies, then as now, to my readers, some of whom were astounded by my decision to withdraw it but accepted it as a writer's eccentricity.

The work now returns in the capable and caring hands of Aleph Book Company, and its managing editor, Aienla Ozukum, who read a copy I sent her, and in a few short days returned with one word of praise, 'terrific'; and an immediate offer to publish with the title I had thought suitable in the first place and with an absolutely arresting cover designed by Bena Sareen.

I have published several books since *Once Upon a...* was released in late 2008, but the prospect of Tony Calangute journeying afresh has suffused me with vindication and satisfaction, which is, along with readers, the lifeblood of writers now leave it to you, dear readers, to take *Tony Calangute* where you will.

Meanwhile, as self-professed paradises continue on their suicidal journeys as paradises all too often do, a change of avatars for the book does not preclude my gratitude to those who helped tell the tale then. That gratitude remains undiminished with *Tony Calangute*.

Hartman de Souza and Ujjwala Samarth introduced me to the Goan soul a lifetime ago, in the 1980s, in a New Delhi barsati they called home at the time. I've been besotted ever since. Aparanta/Goa for me evolved from a place of vacation magic to everyday discovery. It is now home.

This work is in some ways a tribute to Norman Dantas, who lived and died a warrior, and who absorbed fully, though inadvertently, the meaning of the Japanese saying 'nobility of failure'.

Hartman introduced me to the anthemic toast, 'Confusion to our Enemies'. Alistair Miranda contributed a charming phrase from a Goan saxophonist in *Gomantak Times*. Ritu Nanda, Devika Sequeira and Javed Ansari too contributed an arresting term each that I gratefully wove into the tale.

Marius and Medha Monteiro explained Goa to me over priceless hours, and with their now-departed friend and comrade Norman de Souza, engaged me in a delightful course of Konknni phraseology. They also aided in translation.

I again thank Gilda Mendonsa for writing *The Best of Goan Cooking* and Melanie Sequeira for compiling *Food Stop*. From both I learned the joys of Goan cuisine. (The Professor, Lumena and Carla Almeida thank them as well.)

Sérgio Mascarenhas de Almeida, former Director of Delegation in India of Fundação Oriente, friend, unwavering critic and unswerving supporter in my quest for ever better Pasteis de Nata, that food of the gods, helped with translations from Portuguese. Professor Glenn J. Ames, formerly of the University of Toledo shared some of his research and insights into Portuguese colonial history. As with Sérgio, Glenn was a neighbour during my several years of residence on a hilltop in Panjim. Glenn was fatally afflicted with cancer soon after his return to America. We think often of Glenn and his charming family.

Muito obrigado.

Dev Borem Korum.